Trace Stevens ha
four years ago.

He was still sexy as hell and made her body do crazy, previously unexperienced things.

Made her mind go back to the night of passion four years ago that had led to her becoming a single mother by a man she'd just met.

A man who had no idea he'd fathered a son.

Her son. Her sweet, wonderful Joss.

Chrissie swallowed the lump in her throat and prepared herself for what she hadn't really thought would ever happen.

She wasn't supposed to see Trace again.

He wasn't supposed to be here.

Dear Reader,

While writing my last Medical Romance, I became more and more intrigued by my heroine's best friend. By the end of that book, I knew I had to write her story and give her a happy ending.

Chrissie Tomberlain has a secret she's kept for the four years since she last saw Trace Stevens— a beautiful three-year-old son. Providing medical care to impoverished and war-torn countries is Trace's life mission, but he's back in Atlanta for a few weeks and discovers the attraction between him and Chrissie has only grown with time. Trace knows he won't stay and Chrissie isn't looking to have an affair. And when he learns her reasons why, he's confronted with a past he'd rather forget.

I hope you enjoy Trace and Chrissie's book as much as I enjoyed researching and writing their story. Drop me an email at janice@janicelynn.net to share your thoughts about their romance, Chattanooga or just to say hello.

Happy reading,

Janice

THE DOCTOR'S
SECRET SON

———

JANICE LYNN

⟨H⟩HARLEQUIN® MEDICAL ROMANCE™

Recycling programs
for this product may
not exist in your area.

ISBN-13: 978-0-373-21540-9

The Doctor's Secret Son

First North American Publication 2017

Copyright © 2017 by Janice Lynn

Printed in U.S.A.

www.Harlequin.com

Books by Janice Lynn

Harlequin Medical Romance

Flirting with the Doc of Her Dreams
New York Doc to Blushing Bride
Winter Wedding in Vegas
Sizzling Nights with Dr. Off-Limits
It Started at Christmas…
The Nurse's Baby Secret

Visit the Author Profile page
at Harlequin.com for more titles.

Janice won the National Readers' Choice Award for her first book, *The Doctor's Pregnancy Bombshell*.

To my editor, Kathryn Cheshire. Thanks for all your fabulous insight and hard work to make my stories shine.

CHAPTER ONE

IT WAS HER.

Her hair was longer and her body a bit curvier, but the wide smile on her full lips was the same, as was the sparkle in her bright green gaze.

Not for a single second did Dr. Trace Stevens doubt the perky little blonde nurse's identity. How could he? No woman had ever caused such an intense sexual reaction in him as Chrissie Tomberlain.

Trace's lips curved.

This weekend had definitely just taken a turn for the better. A big turn. Four years ago she'd made his last weekend in the States unforgettable. He still had a few weeks before leaving again, but he welcomed the distraction.

Chrissie had been the best distraction he'd ever known.

So much so that even now, from time to time, he'd awaken drenched in sweat, with an ache in his gut that hadn't been satisfied in years.

Four years, to be exact.

Ironic to run into her because more than once he'd considered looking her up, seeing if she was single, seeing if she'd be interested in spending time with him while he was home.

Then again, this event was where they'd met, so

maybe not so ironic. Still, this weekend was exactly what he needed in so many ways.

A few weeks from now, he'd go back to doing what he was meant to do in life. There were places in the world that needed him a lot more than he was needed in Atlanta, Georgia, even if his friends and family thought otherwise.

Chrissie Tomberlain hadn't spent a night away from her three-year-old son since he'd been born. So why had she let her best friend convince her that staying away from him for a whole weekend would be a good idea?

Okay, Savannah was right that Chrissie never did anything but work and take care of Joss. But there wasn't anything she'd rather do than spend time with her son, so she hadn't seen it as a problem. Spending time with Joss was a blessing she cherished each and every time she looked into his precious face, heard his sweet voice, felt his little hands pat her cheek.

Prior to Joss's birth, she had enjoyed volunteering at various charity fund-raisers around her hometown of Chattanooga. She'd done so at the huge children's cancer prevention event in Atlanta several times in the past.

But not since she'd gotten pregnant with Joss.

At the event.

By a man she hadn't seen since.

Until now.

Trace Stevens hadn't changed much from four years ago.

He was still sexy as hell and made her body do crazy, previously unexperienced things.

Made her mind go back to the night of passion of four years ago that had led to her becoming a single mother by a man she'd just met.

A man who had no idea he'd fathered a son.

Her son. Her sweet, wonderful Joss.

She swallowed the lump in her throat and prepared herself for what she hadn't really thought would ever happen.

She wasn't supposed to see Trace again.

He wasn't supposed to be here.

Yet, if she was honest with herself, wouldn't she admit that from the moment she'd gotten into her car in Chattanooga she'd had a nervous energy inside, wondering "what if" the entire two-hour drive?

What if Trace was there?

What if their paths really did cross again?

What if he still lit her body on fire with a mere glance, something no one else had ever done before or since?

There he was, standing in a tent not so unlike the one they'd met in four years ago. For all she knew it might be the exact same one if Children's Cancer Prevention Organization owned their commercial tents, rather than rented them.

A big sexy grin climbed up Trace's face as his gaze collided with hers and recognition hit.

He remembered her.

Of course he remembered her.

They'd spent an entire weekend together. A lot of it *together* together. Four years wasn't so long ago that he'd forget a weekend that hot and heavy.

Then again, maybe he had hot and heavy weekends like that routinely.

She knew nothing about the man except that he was amazing in bed and had been a fellow volunteer at the CCPO. That year, the event had done a three-day walk. This year, the organization was sponsoring a weekend of family fun. On Friday evening, they were having a welcome event and a bubble-a-thon dance party open to all participants and their families. On Saturday morning, they were having a marathon, with various levels of participation. Some committing to a five K, some to the full marathon. Others committing to various distances in between. Then, in the evening, they were having sponsored Olympic-style games for the kids.

Now, as then, Chrissie had signed up to work the medical tent all weekend. Full of nervous energy, she'd dropped Joss off to Savannah early that morning, then made the drive so she could help organize the medical station and volunteer to assist with anything else needed prior to the families and fund-raiser participants starting to arrive.

Imagine running into Trace within minutes of her arrival.

Imagine, she had.

For four years she'd imagined this moment, coming face to face with the man who'd haunted her dreams and her reality.

Yet it wasn't really as intense as it should have been. The sun hadn't stood still in the sky. The earth hadn't quaked. Lightning hadn't streaked its way to the ground. Nothing. They were just standing in a tent, looking at each other, a man and a woman with a past while the rest of the world went on as usual.

No big deal. But her heart pounded like crazy and her chest wanted to heave from lack of air.

Probably had something to do with the look in Trace's eyes when he'd spotted her that said he'd figured out exactly what he'd be doing this weekend, other than working the medical tent.

Or more like who.

Why, oh, why was everything in her screaming *yes*?

Other than her brain, that was. Her brain warned she'd best stay far, far away because to have anything to do with him would be risking everything.

He wasn't that good in bed.

She skimmed her gaze over his body, noting on closer inspection that he was slightly leaner than she remembered, more tan, too. His loose CCPO event T-shirt and khaki cargo shorts did little to hide his broad shoulders and narrow hips. His left hand was still bare of jewelry and had no telltale tan line to hint at deception. Lifting her gaze back to his face, she took in his sandy-colored hair, strong aquiline nose, cleft chin, and toffee-colored eyes that were staring straight into hers with obvious interest. His smile widened and her thighs clenched in immediate response.

He *had* been that good, but she still wasn't risking it.

She had too much at stake to play sexual escapades with Trace all weekend.

But boy, oh, boy, did the man tempt everything in her.

"It's been a while," Trace said by way of greeting when he closed the distance between them.

"Four years."

Four years. Four long years where he'd seen things he'd like to forget, and she was just the woman who might accomplish that for him, even if only for a short while.

A short while sounded like heaven after the hell he'd seen, that he'd no doubt see more of when he returned to wherever they sent him this time.

"How have you been?" he asked, studying her. Other than the change of hairstyle and the few extra pounds she carried, she looked the same as he recalled. Better even. He liked the fullness to her breasts and hips that hadn't been there four years ago.

His groin tightened.

Yeah, he liked her curves a lot.

His body's instant reaction to her nearness made him feel like a Neanderthal. It hadn't been that long since he'd been with a woman. But when he tried to think back to the last time he'd had sex, he struggled to recall exactly how long it had been.

A problem he intended to rectify, assuming Chrissie still felt the strong attraction they'd shared. Time certainly hadn't faded a thing for him.

Sex just hadn't been a priority recently. Life— life had been the top priority where he'd been. Helping those who desperately needed help and doing what he could with significantly limited resources had been a priority. Surviving tragedy, and healing, had been a priority.

"I'm great," she answered, shifting her weight as if she was nervous.

She had nothing to be nervous about. They'd ended on good terms, or so he'd thought, after their weekend. He'd thought about her often enough that had there been anything negative he would have remembered. He'd swear he recalled every detail of that weekend in vivid color.

"That's good to hear. How's life been treating you?"

Her gaze cut to beyond him, and, ignoring his question, she said, "Sorry, but if you'll excuse me, I see someone I need to talk to." She paused, briefly met his gaze with a steely expression in her green eyes. "Good to see you again, Travis."

Travis? Ouch.

He watched her walk away, greet Agnes Coulson, a bear of a woman and the Children's Cancer Prevention Organization founder. True to how he'd just thought of her, Agnes wrapped Chrissie into a big hug, causing her to laugh as she hugged the woman back, then wiggled free.

"It's so good to see you," she exclaimed to the woman, showing the excitement Trace would like to have seen when she'd greeted him. He wouldn't have minded one of those hugs, either.

Instead, he'd effectively been put in his place.

Not that he was buying that she'd forgotten his name.

He wasn't.

She hadn't forgotten. But she wanted him to think she had. That was her way of letting him know she wasn't interested.

Which wasn't what her eyes had conveyed when she'd first seen him. He'd have bet anything she'd felt the same excitement he had.

He knew she had.

Maybe she'd taken that closer look, seen the harshness that almost suffocated him these days, and known the best thing she could do was stay away.

He wasn't the same man he'd been four years

ago. Not by far. In some ways, he was better. In some, not so much.

"You two had something a few years back, didn't you? Right before you left for Sudan?"

Trace turned to Bud Coulson, Agnes's husband. They headed up the event each year. They'd done so for the past twenty years. Their only child had been diagnosed with, and died from, a rare type of brain cancer, and they'd dedicated their lives to raising awareness and funds to fight pediatric cancers. Trace's family regularly donated to their organization. Four years ago, before he'd left for his Doctors Around the World stint overseas, Trace had done more than pull out his hefty checkbook. He'd volunteered as an extra helper, something he'd done numerous times over the years in different capacities with CCPO.

Even before Doctors Around the World he'd wanted to do more to help others than just practice medicine. Thank goodness for Bud and Agnes's influence over the years that had planted that seed that drove him to help others.

How could he not support the foundation when it was a way of keeping Kerry alive to the couple he loved so much?

"I was quite taken with her the weekend we met," he admitted, not letting his mind go to little Kerry and the guilt he always felt when he thought of her.

Instead, he let memories of Chrissie flood

through his mind. He'd always wondered if the intensity of that weekend had been because he'd known he was heading into the unknown. Which he'd wanted. He still wanted even if his parents had begged him to come home to stay. He understood their concern.

Especially after the incident at the Shiara MSF hospital in Yemen.

Automatically, he placed his hand over his right lower abdomen. That one had been a bit too close for comfort, but at least he'd walked away with his life, which he couldn't say of all his colleagues.

Damn cowardly terrorists attacking a hospital. Damn that he'd walked away when so many good people had died.

"Your dad told me about what happened." Bud gestured to where Trace touched. "You should have come home to let us take care of you."

Trace rammed his hand into his pocket.

"There was nothing anyone could do." There hadn't been. He'd been one of the lucky ones. "Besides, I lived."

"I was surprised you didn't opt to come home after that," Bud mused, then shook his head. "I take that back. That you opted to stay didn't really surprise me."

"Coming home wasn't an option." Not one that he'd ever considered at any rate. He planned to live his life doing mission work. Settling down wasn't for him. A wife and kids wasn't his lot in life and he never wanted it to be.

His gaze cut to the woman still smiling and chatting with Agnes. Her hands waved animatedly as she described something. Both women burst into laughter and a deep ache pierced Trace.

"Your father would move heaven and earth to convince you to come back," Bud mused, watching Trace rather than his wife and Chrissie. "He's hoping you're home to stay."

Trace frowned. "We both know I'll be leaving as soon as I'm given my next assignment. My father doesn't understand."

Bud shook his head. "You're right. He doesn't. Not many do."

Trace's eyes shifted toward the older man. "You saying you don't? Because I wouldn't believe you. You of all people understand the need to do more than just accept things for the way they are. This organization is testament to that."

"Agnes and CCPO are my life." One side of Bud's mouth tugged upward. "Then again, at one time the Marine Corps was my life, too. I served time overseas and wouldn't trade those memories and the brothers I gained for anything. I think we accomplished a lot of good things, but that doesn't mean I'd go back. Sometimes we have to let go of one thing we care about to make room for another." He glanced lovingly at his wife.

Trace cocked his brow at the older man. "You trying to tell me you don't think I should go?"

Bud shrugged. "Only you know the answer to whether or not you should go back." He nodded toward where Chrissie and Agnes still talked, obviously catching up. "Maybe it's time you find a reason to want to stay home rather than go as far away as possible."

"Those people need help every bit as much as the kids you're raising money for," Trace pointed out, not acknowledging Bud's claim that he might have been running from something when he'd signed on to Doctors Around the World. "They're innocent victims of governments and wars they have no control over."

"Civilians are always the innocent victims of war," Bud agreed. "You do what you feel is right for you, son. All I'm saying is that there is a lot of good you can do here, too. I just think you need to keep that in mind, because I'm not convinced going back is the right choice for you."

Trace eyed the older man suspiciously. "You're sure Dad didn't put you up to trying to talk me into staying?"

Bud laughed. "I won't say he's never mentioned hoping you'd stay to me, but I'm speaking for myself."

Trace nodded. He'd figured as much. His successful businessman father would probably fund

Bud's charity for the next fifty years if he could convince Trace to stay in Atlanta.

Which would be a good reason to stay, if it didn't mean having to deal with his father on a regular basis.

"In case you haven't noticed, Blondie is looking your way."

Trace had noticed. Hard not to notice those intense emerald eyes studying him. He could feel her interest, could feel her body's reaction to him.

The same interest and reaction he was having to her.

Obviously, the chemistry they'd shared still burned hot.

So, why had she given him the cold shoulder?

Chrissie ordered her gaze to remove itself from Trace. Unfortunately, her eyes didn't seem connected to her brain.

Why did he have to be so hot? Those amazing eyes just sucked her in. Rich, warm toffee that made her want to melt.

She was melting.

No wonder she'd lost her mind four years ago. Trace was hot. Scorching, melt-a-woman-all-the-way-to-her-toes hot.

Chrissie's toes were ooey-gooey puddles in her shoes.

"It's good to have Trace back with us, too, isn't it?"

Oops. Obviously, Agnes noticed her distraction and had no compunction on commenting.

Chrissie dragged her gaze away from Trace and focused on the older woman, who was watching her curiously. Something told her the woman wouldn't buy it if she pretended not to know what she referred to. After all, Chrissie and Trace had only had eyes for each other four years ago. No doubt every volunteer there had picked up on their attraction.

"Where's he been?" she asked.

Agnes's concerned gaze went to Trace. "For the past couple of years? Yemen."

Surprise hit Chrissie. "Yemen?"

"He works with Doctors Around the World." A troubled look came over Agnes's face, making her appear every one of her sixty plus years. "He'll be leaving again soon. Unfortunately. He's home because his only cousin had a baby and the timing fell right at the end of his contract."

Chrissie's gaze went back to Trace. Yemen. She knew that was in the Middle East, but she wasn't sure exactly where. She probably should have paid better attention in geography class.

"I wondered if you two had stayed in touch while he was there and that it wasn't a coincidence you were both volunteering again at the same time." Agnes looked disappointed. "Obviously not."

Chrissie shook her head. "No, meeting Trace four years ago was nice." Nice? Ha, that was so not the right word to describe that meeting. More like naughty. "But neither of us fooled each other that our meeting was anything more. I didn't know he'd be here."

"Too bad," Agnes countered. "That boy needs someone in his life."

"You sound as if you know him well," Chrissie mused, trying not to look overly interested.

"All his life. His father and Bud go back a long way. Well," she clarified with a low laugh, "all the way back to elementary school. They were best friends. Trace was a few months older than our daughter. We'd always hoped they'd grow up, fall in love, and connect our families in yet another way." Pain momentarily aged her face. "Instead, Kerry died and Trace spends his time overseas."

"Are you gossiping about me, Agnes?"

Agnes quickly recovered, her cheeks turning a rosy pink. "Every chance I get to extol your virtues."

"My virtues don't deserve extolling."

There was more to what he was saying than what appeared. But Chrissie's own cheeks were burning too much with embarrassment at getting caught discussing him for her to over-analyze his comment.

"That's a matter of opinion," Agnes countered. "So, where are we going to put our Chrissie to work this year?"

Chrissie frowned. She wasn't their Chrissie. At

least, not *his* Chrissie. But Agnes was smiling and chatting on about the medical tent and making sure everything was ready for the event kick-off.

"I'd like to do triage if that's okay," Chrissie spoke up. "It's what I did last time."

"You've been back?" Trace asked, studying her.

Agnes nodded. "Not for a few years, but our Chrissie is an angel from heaven, for sure."

Yeah, Chrissie was pretty sure with the way her insides were burning that she was from somewhere way more south.

And Agnes knew that it had been four years. Why had she left the date a little vague?

"Maybe you could take her to the triage area and show her how things are set up this year?" Agnes's question was directed at Trace.

"Yes, ma'am." His gaze locked with Chrissie's and he grinned as if she hadn't cut him off earlier. "Follow me."

His facial expression was so similar to one she often saw on her son's face that her breath caught. Her feet refused to move. Her head spun.

"Chrissie?"

Shaking her head to stop the spinning, she stepped toward him.

Three days. Three days and then she'd change charities to volunteer at ones in Chattanooga so she'd never have to see Trace Stevens again.

CHAPTER TWO

"You've changed."

Chrissie's gaze shot to Trace's. Of course she had changed. She was a mother now. Not that she was going to tell him that.

Although they hadn't done a lot of talking four years ago, he had told her that he was a bachelor for life and had no plans to reproduce ever. Because of his words, and the trauma from her parents' custody battle when she was seven, Chrissie had convinced herself that Joss belonged to her because she'd just been a weekend fling for Trace.

Guilt pinched at her conscience, but she shoved it aside.

Now was not the time to feel guilty. They'd shared a wild weekend of sex that had never been meant to be anything more. He hadn't wanted it to be anything more.

Only she'd ended up pregnant.

Pregnant, and she hadn't known how to get in touch with him.

She could have contacted Bud and Agnes, could have asked for Trace's information. Perhaps they would have given it to her.

Only, she hadn't.

She and Trace had parted ways with no plans to stay in touch or ever see each other again. He'd known the city where she lived because she'd told him. Just as he'd told her he lived in Atlanta. He hadn't bothered to get in touch with her or continue their relationship in any way.

If he'd left the country, who knew if he'd even had a way of staying in touch? Then again, if he'd wanted to, he would have found a way. Chattanooga wasn't that big and tracking down a nurse with her name couldn't have been that difficult.

He hadn't, and because of that she'd never felt the need to attempt to track him down. Well, twinges from time to time, but overall she knew she'd done the right thing for her son and had even given Trace what he'd said he wanted by keeping her secret.

How Joss had come into existence didn't matter these days. What mattered was her precious little boy who was the center of her world, and that she'd do anything to protect him from the hell she'd gone through as a child. She would give him the best life possible, and that was that.

But then, she hadn't thought she'd see Trace again. Not really.

She stared into his eyes, wondering at the emotions she saw flickering there.

She hadn't known he was leaving the country, hadn't known he was with Doctors Around the World. He'd never mentioned anything of the sort to her. Something like leaving the country for an extended period of time was a big deal.

"When did you leave for Doctors Around the World?"

His pupils dilated and for the briefest moment darkness replaced the interest in his eyes. "I see Agnes really was gossiping about me."

He hadn't answered her question. Interesting. Most of the guys she knew would have made sure everyone knew they were a doctor, that they'd signed up selflessly to help others, and they'd have played that angle to the max. Four years ago Trace hadn't told her he was a doctor or that he was with DAW.

Fifteen minutes and she already knew things about him she hadn't known then.

Was that why he'd told her he wasn't interested in anything more than a weekend fling and never would be? Because he'd been about to leave?

"When?" she repeated, needing to know, although she wasn't sure why it even mattered. That he hadn't told her such pertinent details about his life just reinforced what she already knew. It hadn't mattered that she hadn't known the details of his life. She was not someone who mattered.

"The week after we met." His lips twisted as if the words triggered unpleasant memories. "I'd purposely put off my leave date until after the event so I could help Bud and Agnes and to spend a little time with them before I took off. That's why I didn't sign on to work as a physician at the event, but just as extra help where needed."

The week after... He'd left the country the week after they'd met.

"I haven't been back in the United States since. Not until a week ago."

Four years had passed and he'd not come home. For all of Joss's life, Trace had been out of the country, serving others.

"Oh."

"Yeah, oh." He reached out, brushed his fingertip over her cheek then down her jawline. "Not sure how much help I was that weekend. All I remember about those three days is you."

Her insides perked up at his admission and it was all she could do not to ask "It is?" with a silly school girl expression plastered to her face. Instead, she bit her tongue.

He'd been out of the country for four years. How many times while she'd been pregnant had she thought about him living it up in Atlanta's night life? Wining and dining some slim beauty queen while she grew rounder and rounder with his child? The glimpse of darkness in his eyes said that he hadn't been wining or dining anyone, that he'd seen things he'd like to forget, that the past four years hadn't been a bed of roses.

"Have you thought about me, Chrissie?"

She winced. Had he read her mind?

Still, she didn't want to answer his question any more than he'd wanted to answer hers. She didn't want to tell him that not a day went by that he didn't cross her mind.

How could it when Joss was a constant reminder?

When she went home, it would be even worse now that she'd seen Trace again and realized just how much her son truly resembled his handsome father. The facial expressions. The eyes. Joss was Trace's mini-me.

"Or did you forget me the minute you left Atlanta?"

His question made her sound as if she had flings all the time, as if what she'd done with him had been no big deal. Other than a college boyfriend she'd hung around with long enough for him to take her virginity and introduce her to a mediocre sex life, she'd had no other lovers. Only Trace.

There had been nothing mediocre about Trace.

But she wasn't telling him that, either.

Because he'd been so good he must have had many lovers over the years.

Had probably had many since, despite his being out of the country. Chrissie couldn't suppress her grimace.

"You know as well as I do that you aren't exactly the kind of man a woman forgets," she admitted as if it were no big deal. "Nor was that weekend the kind I'd just forget."

"Good to know." He smiled at her admission. "It was a phenomenal weekend, wasn't it?"

She crossed her arms and kept her mouth shut. She'd answered enough questions.

"But not one you want to repeat?"

Yeah, she didn't want to answer that either. Mainly because her body was like, "Yes, sign me up for an encore performance!" but her brain knew the best thing she could do was keep as much distance between her and Trace as possible.

He was the father to her son. A son he didn't know about. She needed to stay far, far away before she slipped up and said something she shouldn't. What if she said something and he pulled a stunt like the one her father had pulled?

She couldn't bear the thought of Trace disappearing with her son. Not that he would likely even want anything to do with Joss, but, still, her own father had practically ignored her the first seven years of her life and that hadn't stopped him.

Her gaze lifted to his and rather than saying, *No, I don't want a repeat*, as a good, smart girl would do, she asked, "Why do you say that?"

His expression brightened. "Then you do want a repeat?"

Ugh. She'd walked right into that one.

She studied his toffee-colored gaze, his smooth tanned skin, the obvious sexual interest in his eyes. "You do?"

"What sane man wouldn't want a repeat of what you and I had?"

There was that.

"Sex without strings?"

His gaze narrowed. "Not exactly how I'd have worded it."

She didn't let her gaze waver. "Which doesn't make it any less true."

His forehead furrowed and he did some studying of his own. She refused to look away, refused to shift her weight or show any sign of weakness.

Even if her insides quaked at the power this man had over her.

"Did you want strings, Chrissie?"

Heat rushed into her face. She was going to have to be careful of what she said. Which was why she needed to stay away. Nothing good could come from spending time with Trace.

"No, of course not." She hadn't. She'd known what they shared was just a man and a woman thrown together by circumstances and sexual attraction. "You told me you weren't the marrying kind. I didn't expect anything to come of our weekend together." She sure hadn't expected to become a mother. "No strings was fine."

A tired look came over his face and he raked his fingers through his hair. "I was leaving the country in three days. I couldn't have done strings if I'd wanted to."

Something in his tone had her insides fluttering with a bundle of nervous energy.

"Did you want to?"

* * *

Good question, and one that Trace had asked himself a thousand times in the years that had passed since he'd last seen this woman. What would he have done differently had he not been committed?

"I didn't allow myself to consider strings as a possibility." Which was what he always came back to when his mind got to wondering. Not that he would ever have settled down, but he would have liked more time with Chrissie, to have been able to let the fire between them burn out naturally.

Her pretty face pinched and her gaze averted. "Which explains why you never asked for a phone number."

Although he was sure she didn't want them to, her words conveyed that she'd been hurt. That he'd hurt her stung.

"There was no point in my asking."

"I see." Her lower lip disappeared again.

"I don't think you do." He lifted her chin and stared into the greenest eyes he'd ever looked into. "I was leaving the country, had volunteered for a crazy assignment. Putting you or any woman through the stress of a relationship when I was over there, especially when nothing would ever have come from that relationship anyway—it wouldn't have been fair."

Her chin trembled beneath his fingertips and Trace wanted to kiss her so badly his insides ached. They were alone in the medical tent, but someone could walk in. Which didn't overly concern him. He'd seen and done too much to let something as irrelevant as someone seeing him kiss Chrissie get to him. But Chrissie was still sending mixed signals.

One minute hot, the next cold.

When he kissed her next, he wanted her to want it as much as he did, not to be second-guessing herself.

He would kiss her again. Soon. She might not want to admit it, but she wanted the kiss as much as he did. Everything in her expression, her stance, her eyes, said so.

"Well, I guess you're a damn saint, then, eh?"

There went the cold again. And the hurt.

"Far from it."

Looking away, she shrugged. "Not to hear Agnes tell it."

"Agnes is biased. She's my godmother."

Chrissie's eyes widened. Obviously Agnes hadn't told her that part.

"Her husband, Bud, and my father grew up in the same neighborhood and were best friends. Somehow, that friendship survived my father's personality all these years."

"Something wrong with your father's personality?"

Ha, now there was a tricky question if ever there was one.

"Most people would say he's near perfect."

Her eyebrow arched. "But not you?"

Not a subject he wanted to discuss any more than he wanted to discuss Sudan or Yemen or Kerry. Maybe less so.

"So, about those Braves…"

He watched emotions play across her face, but she let any further questions she had go. How many times had he closed his eyes and recalled her face? How many times when the whole world seemed to have gone crazy had he closed his eyes and just remembered everything about her?

"Yeah, well, apparently you don't recall, or maybe you never knew—" her chin tilted upward "—but I'm not a fan of baseball."

Well, no one was perfect even if in his mind she was close.

"That's un-American," he teased.

She shrugged. "Overpaid bunch of men who never grew up as far as I'm concerned."

His lips twitched. "I'll have you know those guys work hard."

She gave him an accusing look. "You sound as if you're one of them. Former player or just a wannabe?"

He laughed and it felt good. Foreign, but good. He'd not had many reasons to laugh over the past four years. It hadn't all been bad. Some parts had been wonderful. He'd been helping people who desperately needed help. But overall there hadn't been nearly enough laughter.

For all the craziness, he'd felt as if he was doing something positive in the world, had felt alive and needed.

"Nope, never been much of a baseball player," he admitted. "But I have a few friends on the team."

"On the Atlanta Braves baseball team?" She sounded incredulous.

He nodded. His father handled more than one of the players' finances, was a real-estate mogul, and prior to Trace leaving the country they'd moved in the same social circles. These days, all the parties and hoopla seemed pointless when there were people starving and being killed for their beliefs or place of birth.

Shaking off the memory, he focused on the petite blonde staring up at him and drank her in like a breath of fresh air.

Chrissie's brows pinched. "Just who are you, anyway?"

Determined that he was going to keep the past four years at bay, not think about pending decisions that needed making about his future, Trace grinned. "That's right. You forgot my name."

For the first time, a smile toyed on her lips.

A guilty smile.

That she'd pretended not to remember him was as telling as her comment about his not asking for her phone number.

He stuck out his hand. "Hi. I'm Trace Stevens.

I'm a volunteer in the medical tent. I'll be working closely with you over the next couple of days."

"Not that closely."

It occurred to him that just because his life
hadn't moved forward, a lot could have changed
in hers.

He'd just assumed she was single, available.

His gaze dropped to her left hand and specifically to her empty third finger.

"No wedding ring," he mused out loud. "Boyfriend?"

"I'm not married." Her lower lip disappeared
between her teeth. "But I date from time to time."

He let her answer digest, not liking the green
sludge making its way through his veins. He had
no claims on her. He never had. When he'd spotted her across the tent he hadn't even considered
that she might be involved with someone else. He'd
just seen her and wanted her.

Four years had come and gone. It wasn't as if
he'd have expected anyone to have waited on him.

And to wait for what? A weekend fling every
few years when he came home?

He had nothing to offer beyond that and never
would.

CHAPTER THREE

CHRISSIE NEEDED TO get away from Trace. Quickly. Being around him made her insides mush.

"So," she said as a way of moving the conversation away from anything personal. "What can I do to help get things set up?"

"Bud and Agnes are so organized they have most everything taken care of. The bins of donated supplies are over here and are labeled. We can set the area up along the lines of what we did four years ago."

Chrissie's face heated, which told her way too much about her state of mind.

"A triage area and a treatment area?" Had her voice been several octaves higher or was that just her imagination?

"Yes." How dared he sound so calm? "We'll set one treatment area up to be a bit more private, just in case."

No. No. No. There went her naughty imagination again to places it shouldn't go. To memories of a former private treatment area where her body had been quite ravished.

She couldn't prevent her blush.

Hoping he didn't notice, or that he'd think it the result of the Georgia heat, she nodded. "That works for me. How many volunteers do we have in the medical area this year?"

The more the better. She hoped they were so over-staffed that being alone was impossible.

"Around a dozen, I think." He pulled out a list and began reading it. "We have a couple of doctors, a couple of nurses, a paramedic, a few nurse practitioners, and a few techs, and then some med and nursing students. It should run smoothly."

"Trace Stevens, is that you?" a female voice with a light accent called out from the other side of the tent.

Trace and Chrissie both turned. A pretty brunette with long sleek hair pulled into a ponytail headed their direction. A huge smile was on her face and Chrissie wouldn't have been surprised if she'd broken into a run to close the gap between her and Trace quicker.

"Alexis," he greeted the woman, who wrapped her arms around him and gave him a big hug. "I just saw your name on the list."

Chrissie was beginning to think she was going to have to peel the woman off to get her to let go of Trace, but eventually, and with obvious reluctance, she stepped back and brushed her hands down her white shorts and turquoise top.

"I heard you were back in town—" Alexis's smile was so big and bright she could be a toothpaste ad "—and would be here this weekend, but thought it too good to be true."

"You heard right." Trace grinned easily at the beautiful woman.

No wonder. She was a Greek goddess, had a husky voice that held a light accent and was downright sexy, and she was looking at Trace with obvious interest in her dark eyes.

She was looking at him the way Chrissie had, no doubt, looked at him four years ago.

Thank goodness she wasn't looking at him that way now. Okay, maybe a little.

I am not jealous, she told herself over and over. *It does not matter that another woman is batting her lashes at him as if he is coated in chocolate and she's just come off a strict diet.*

It didn't matter. He meant nothing to Chrissie. Just a stranger she'd had an amazing weekend with years ago.

A stranger who she'd made a child with.

She grimaced. Yeah, there was that. Which explained why she couldn't bear to watch their interaction a moment longer. It had nothing to do with anything other than a natural instinct because of Joss.

"Um…I'll go unpack bins while you two catch up," she offered, not even sure if either of them remembered she was there as the woman caught him up on a few mutual acquaintances and their recent activities.

At Chrissie's words, the woman gave a horrified look. "Did I interrupt? I'm sorry. I saw Trace and had to immediately say hello and then, as always with this man, I got carried away." She winked at Chrissie as if they shared a secret. "He has that effect on women, so be careful."

Chrissie didn't need Alexis to point out the effect Trace had on women. She knew. She forced a smile, tight though it was, to her lips.

"I'll take note."

"Chrissie's immune to whatever effect I have," he told Alexis, although Chrissie had no idea why.

The woman's perfectly shaped eyebrow arched.

Chrissie frowned, but didn't respond to his comment.

Trace's gaze darted back and forth between the gorgeous brunette and Chrissie. No doubt he saw the stark contrast. It was hard to miss.

"Chrissie, this is Dr. Alexis Gianakos," Trace introduced the woman. "One of the best cardiologists I've ever had the pleasure of working with."

A doctor? Beautiful *and* smart it would seem.

"As you may have figured out from our conversation, she and I worked at the same hospital prior to when I joined DAW," Trace continued. "She's volunteering this weekend."

Will you be working closely with her, too? Chrissie wanted to ask, but somehow managed to keep her tongue in place.

Ugh. She hated feeling jealous. Hated it.

But she was. Denial didn't make reality any less true.

"Nice to meet you," she greeted, holding out her hand and forcing the corners of her mouth upward.

The woman took her hand. Hers was smooth, strong, feminine. Well-manicured.

Chrissie couldn't help but look down at her own as she pulled away from the woman's. A bit rough, nails cropped short and unpainted, and no jewelry.

None on the horizon, either.

She'd dated, but found she quickly tired of the men who had come into her life. They either thought because she was a single mom that that meant she was easy for the taking or they didn't understand that Joss came first and always would. None had lasted beyond a couple of dates.

Her best friend, Savannah, was always pushing her to date, especially now that Savannah was so over the moon, happily married to cardiologist Dr. Charlie Keele. Just because Savannah had found the right man for her it didn't mean Chrissie had to do the same. Or that she even wanted to. She was quite happy with just her and Joss. Fabulously so.

"You're also an old friend of Trace's?" Alexis's accent came out a bit thicker than previously.

"We aren't old friends, just acquaintances who met here a few years ago."

"Ah," Alexis said as if gaining insight. This time it was her dark gaze going back and forth between Chrissie and Trace.

"If you'll excuse me, I'll get started," Chrissie said, feeling more and more awkward.

She walked away before either could say anything. She didn't want to listen to the beautiful woman chat up Trace and she sure didn't want to listen to whatever response he made to the woman's obvious interest.

Had they been an item when Trace worked with her? The woman was so beautiful that no doubt they'd made an attractive couple.

He was free to do whatever he wanted. Whomever he wanted. But she didn't want to know about it. Or see it.

What she'd really like to do was block it completely from her mind. Forever. She began organizing supplies and forcing a smile to stay on her face.

Attitude was everything and she was going to have a good attitude this weekend even if it killed her.

Chrissie was jealous.

She had no reason to be jealous, but the fact that she was made Trace happier than it should have.

Alexis was still chatting about the hospital and his former coworkers, but Trace's attention followed Chrissie to where she began opening bins with a vengeance and a smile that didn't fit. He'd already helped volunteers set up tables and chairs in their tent, so, other than however they opted to organize their supplies, there wasn't a lot more to do. Many of their items would stay boxed up until needed.

"Who is she?"

Alexis's question didn't surprise him. Right or wrong, he hadn't attempted to hide his interest in Chrissie.

"I met her here four years ago."

"You stayed in touch?"

Still watching Chrissie work, he shook his head. "I've not seen or spoken to her since until today."

Surprise registered on Alexis's face. "That must have been some meeting four years ago."

"Must have been," was all he said, then, "I'm going to help her set up. You coming?"

Chrissie was one of those people who liked event-opening ceremonies. She liked knowing the history of whatever was taking place, of who the funds were going to help, of who they had already helped. Tonight's was no exception.

Listening to Bud and Agnes talk about their daughter who'd died with cancer at such a young age, of the heartbreaking prevalence of childhood cancers, listening to how they had formed the Children's Cancer Prevention Organization and how the charity had grown, and their hope it would expand further into more cities, filled her heart with warm emotion.

She simply could not imagine something happening to Joss or how she would react if it did. Like Bud and Agnes, she'd like to think she'd deal with her grief in a way that would make the world a better place for others.

She wasn't sure she'd be able to function at all.

"What are you thinking?"

Chrissie jumped at Trace's question. "I didn't see you."

"Obviously." His gaze was on her rather than the stage where Agnes spoke. "You were lost in your thoughts."

"I was marveling at how Bud and Agnes turned something so personally tragic into something so positive."

"They are good people who live to give to others."

"Some would say a man who gave up four years of his life to help others was a good person, too."

His expression tightened. "On my best day I don't measure up to the man and woman on that stage."

"Yeah, well, I didn't say I meant you," Chrissie assured him, grateful when his serious expression lightened at her comment, as she'd intended.

There was something darker about him than she remembered. No doubt the things he'd seen over the past four years had changed him.

Was there anyone in Trace's life that made it better? Someone who helped him deal with the no doubt tragic situations he'd encountered while working overseas?

"Is Alexis an old girlfriend?" That wasn't what she'd meant to ask when she'd opened her mouth.

"We went out a few times."

His smile was quick and too cocky for her liking. He knew she was jealous of the woman. Great.

"Which is more than you can say about me, so I guess that answers my question." Which probably only made her sound jealous and bitter and judgmental. Ugh. She should keep her mouth shut.

"What question would that be?"

"Whether or not you'd slept with her." She fought to keep the image of him with the woman from her mind. An image she'd fought for four years. She'd just never had a face to put with her thoughts of what he'd been doing while she'd been raising their son.

"I haven't."

She rolled her eyes. "Right."

"I said she and I went out a few times. I didn't say we had 'stayed in' a few times." At her continued doubt, he added, "I have no reason to lie to you."

He had a point. He owed her nothing, least of all a defense of whether or not he'd had sex with someone.

"No, I guess you don't," she admitted, trying to hide the fact that she was happy he hadn't slept with the beautiful Alexis.

"Would it matter if I had?"

Good grief. Could he see inside her head or what?

"No." But she was lying. It would have mattered. Maybe it shouldn't, but it would have. Because of Joss, she told herself. That was why she cared who he'd slept with and who he hadn't. Because she'd given birth to his child that made her more possessive, more concerned. At least, that was what she was going to keep telling herself, as she conveniently ignored the fact he'd been out of the country for four years.

Hoping he hadn't realized she'd lied and that if he had, he wouldn't call her on it, Chrissie focused on the stage.

Agnes was still speaking and Chrissie did her best to take in each word. With Trace standing so close, she couldn't focus on the woman on stage. She was surrounded by people. How was it possible to be so physically aware of one man that she could smell his spicy scent, hear the call of his body?

"I don't believe you," Trace whispered close to her ear, further sensitizing her nerve-endings.

His breath tickled her skin. She could feel his heat and would swear he'd just nuzzled her hair.

"It really doesn't matter what you believe," she said, stepping back. "I'll see you in medical."

With that she pushed through the crowd to get away from him.

But mainly to get away from her unwanted re-action to everything about him.

Later that evening in the medical tent, Trace lifted the fifty-year-old woman's foot and examined her swollen ankle.

"Yep." He glanced at her name tag on the lan-yard around her neck. "Ms. Perez, you have defi-nitely done a number on your ankle."

"I shouldn't have been quite so vigorous danc-ing in the bubbles, eh?"

"Apparently not." He had her turn and rest on her knees while he squeezed her calf, watching carefully as it triggered the appropriate movement in her foot. "There's no evidence that you've torn your Achilles' tendon, but you're definitely out of commission for the rest of the weekend."

The woman's face fell. "I was afraid you were going to say that. Can't you give me a quick-fix pill?"

"It's not that easy, Ms. Perez. Some things take time and rest, not a pill. I'm sorry."

She heaved her chest in frustration. "Me, too."

"Sit here with ice for about twenty minutes with your foot elevated. Later, one of the guys will drive you on a gator to your tent. Is there someone we can call for you?"

Ms. Perez shook her head. "My daughter is out of town with work and my son lives in Chicago with his wife and kids. I'm by myself."

He gestured to her leg. "You need to stay off that ankle."

"I was looking forward to volunteering in the food tent. I've not missed a year there since CCPO started these events."

"There's no way I can okay for you to serve food."

The woman perked up. "Maybe I could volunteer in a different way? One where I could still keep my foot up?"

Trace didn't want to burst the woman's bubble, but she was going to be in quite a bit of pain and wouldn't be able to put any weight on her ankle for several days. Not with the amount she'd injured the tissue.

Stepping back into the exam area, Chrissie assisted the woman in propping up her foot and then put the woman's ice pack back on her ankle. "Is there anything I can get you? We have a few magazines if you'd like, and I brought a stack of books I've finished if you want to take one."

The woman shook her head and held up her cellular phone. "I have books on this thing to keep my mind occupied for times such as these."

Patting the woman's hand, Chrissie smiled. "That's good."

The medical tent had been slow most of the evening.

Trace liked being busy, and felt restless. He was used to having more to do than time to do it.

Alexis was seeing a gentleman who had come

into the tent with some indigestion. The other volunteers were not quite twiddling their thumbs but none of them were busy, either.

Trace compared it to where he'd been not so long ago, in the midst of mayhem and a war-torn country where there had been more ill and injured than hands to care for them, with problems much worse than a sprained ankle.

He closed his eyes. There were other assignments he could take with Doctors Around the World. Less dangerous places. He didn't have to go back to the places he'd gone before, but he chose to.

"You okay?"

He opened his eyes, surprised Chrissie had initiated a conversation with him that didn't have something to do with a patient or the event. For the most part she'd ignored him or given him the cold shoulder when he'd attempted conversation.

"Fine."

Appearing torn, she eyed him. "You didn't look fine. You looked like you didn't feel well."

"Had a flashback," he admitted, shocking himself that he'd said the words out loud. He hadn't talked to anyone here about the things he'd seen or done. DAW had required he go through psychological evaluation. He'd passed with flying colors, but that wasn't to say that the things he'd lived through and seen hadn't affected him. He'd never be quite the same. "No big deal."

It wasn't a big deal. Nothing he couldn't cope with.

"What kind of flashback?"

"Not one of you," he teased, unwilling to tell her the nitty-gritty details, "so it wasn't good."

She smirked. "Ha-ha. Too funny. Seriously, you turned a bit green there for a few seconds."

Maybe he'd been green at how stand-offish she was around him. He wanted to go back to the way she was four years ago.

He suddenly longed for at least a glimpse of more carefree times. Even if just a short one.

"You want to go play in the bubbles?"

Her jaw dropped at the same time her brow rose. "What?"

He gestured around the medical tent. "We're not busy and might not get another chance to catch more of the events. The bubbles are new this year. Agnes was excited about them."

The more he said, the more he wanted her to say yes. He wanted to play, to let loose and have fun. With Chrissie.

"But...we can't leave. Ms. Perez," she reminded him, looking a little panicked.

"You should go," the woman called from a few feet away, obviously listening to their conversation. "Don't mind me. I'm fine and can have one of these other folk help me out of here."

First mouthing "thank you," Trace grinned at the woman. "See, Ms. Perez wants us to go check out the bubbles. We'll share a dance in her honor."

"That would be absolutely lovely!" the woman

exclaimed, clapping her hands together and obviously playing cupid. "I insist you go."

Chrissie still looked hesitant.

"Hey, Gianakos?" he called to Alexis, who had just finished with the only other patient in the tent and sent him on his way with an antacid and instructions to cut back on spicy foods. "Will you check on Ms. Perez's ankle in a few? She's got about another ten minutes of icing, then have one of the guys take her to wherever she wants to go. Chrissie and I are going to the main area for a while."

Alexis shot an envious glance toward Chrissie, then nodded. "No problem."

"Perfect. See, I'll be fine." Ms. Perez shooed them away. "You two go have a little fun."

Before she could find another excuse, Trace grabbed Chrissie's hand and led her out of Medical. "Thank you."

"For?"

"Not kicking and screaming the whole way. I needed to get out of there for a few."

She looked as if she still might kick and scream, then her expression morphed into one of confusion. "Trace, what were you thinking about back there?"

He shook his head. "Nothing important now. Let's go check out the bubbles."

Her hand was still inside his. He didn't want to let go so he held on tightly as he led them toward the bubbles. Her hand felt warm and comfortable in his.

As if it belonged there.

Without thought he lifted her hand to his lips and pressed a kiss to the top. Because that felt warm and comfortable, as if it belonged in that moment in time.

"Trace, I…" Chrissie's voice trailed off as she came to an abrupt stop and stared up at him. "You shouldn't."

She was right. He shouldn't, but he was glad he had. They stood behind the medical tent on the path leading toward the main event area. They were alone, but someone could come up the path at any time.

"Probably not." He was only home for a short while, had nothing to offer her beyond the weekend. Which was too bad, because from the time he'd seen her he'd known what he wanted, what he needed. Chrissie.

"Yes."

But her eyes said something different and that fueled him forward to say what had already been in the back of his mind, tempting his conscious thought and actions.

"We were good together. We could be good together again."

Her expression tightened.

And then he'd take off for parts unknown, for who knew how long, before he'd be home for another few weeks' hiatus from his reality? Maybe he should let the attraction go but, for whatever reason, he pushed. Whatever it was about Chrissie seemed to be dictating his every move from the moment he'd laid eyes on her that afternoon.

"I can tell you're still attracted to me," he pointed out, as if that were breaking news.

"Doesn't matter." Her exasperation was palpable, and yet she still didn't pull her hand away from his, just kept staring at where their fingers intertwined.

"Sure, it does." To prove his point, he bent and pressed his lips to hers. Gentle, to where she could push him away with ease if she wanted to.

He hoped she didn't. Her lips were so sweet.

She didn't stop him or push him away, but he felt the struggle within her and that gave him pause.

He pulled back, stared down into her wide eyes.

Her wide, slightly dazed eyes.

Her eyes that were filled with desire so sweet it punched him in the gut.

This was why he hadn't been able to resist kissing her.

Because her kisses were addictive and powerful. He craved what being with her promised.

"You taste good, like the sweetest wine, making me want to drink until I'm intoxicated," he admitted. "Let me, Chrissie. We both know you want to."

CHAPTER FOUR

CHRISSIE STARED UP at the man who had haunted her dreams for four years. Who needed more? One kiss and she already felt drunk.

Because his kiss drugged her and made her forget reason.

She wanted to drag him back to her, to kiss him all over until they were both satiated, until the whole world subsided and it was just the two of them.

As it had felt four years ago.

"What a marvelous event," a woman's voice interrupted as she and a group of women rounded the path.

Tugging her hand free from his, Chrissie stepped back to the side of a tent.

"Absolutely. CCPO fund-raisers are always the best fun," another chimed in.

"The first day and we're already sneaking around in the shadows."

"Which should tell you something."

She sighed. "That I'm crazy?"

"That there's something between us."

More than he knew.

"That doesn't mean we should act on that something," she tried to reason, reminding herself that she had to think of Joss, not her crazy body's reaction to him.

"Should I apologize that I want you still, Chrissie? Do you want me to pretend I don't find you attractive?"

Her heartbeat thundered in her ears. "If I said yes, would you?"

He studied her a moment, then took on a slight look of remorse. "If you said yes."

Say no. Say no. Say no.

Chrissie wasn't sure where the inner voice was coming from, but the phrase beat in perfect rhythm with her racing heart.

"I know you're struggling with this, Chrissie. I see it in your eyes when you look at me. I felt it in your kiss. You wanted to let go and just feel, but wouldn't allow yourself."

He certainly had her pegged.

"My question is why?"

"Been there, done that," she reminded him.

"Was our time together so bad?"

"No, but I'd like to think I've learned a thing or two over the last four years."

"Such as?"

"Such as I shouldn't get mixed up with sexy strangers."

"I'm not a stranger."

"Sure, you are."

His brow inched upward. "You believe that?"

"Yes."

"Then we should get to know each other this weekend."

She narrowed her gaze suspiciously. "To what purpose?"

"To know each other. There doesn't have to be a purpose beyond that."

In the flickering light of the shadows, Chrissie stared at him. Get to know Trace? Why?

What about when Joss asked about his father years down the road?

Simple things like what was his favorite color and had he played sports or had any major childhood illnesses? Shouldn't she know how to answer her son? Wouldn't it be horrible to have to say she didn't know anything beyond the fact that Trace had seemed a likable, good person, and had made her laugh and feel as if she was sexy?

He still made her feel sexy.

Every time his eyes lit on her, they shifted as if molten gold had been poured in their depths. Trace wanted her. Whatever the attraction between them was, it was powerful. The way he looked at her made her feel beautiful, desirable. It was a heady sensation.

"You're talking get to know each other as in not biblically know each other, right?" she clarified.

He chuckled. "Make no mistake, my ultimate goal is to physically 'know you' again. But for the moment, I am talking get to know each other as in not biblically."

She wanted to say yes, but knew she'd be toying with dynamite. "I'm not sure."

"It's obvious you're attracted to me," he pointed out.

"Okay, fine, you're an attractive man and I'm not blind." If not for Joss, would she even be hesitating?

"You're saying any attractive man would do?"

"That's not what I'm saying."

"Then that makes me special?"

More so than he knew.

His look of triumph made her nervous. "Are you fishing for compliments, Trace? Because, if so, you grabbed the wrong woman from the medical tent. Dr. Gianakos would be more than happy to be your fluffer."

At her comment, he grinned and shook his head. "I got the right girl and want her complimenting me. Come on, no more serious talk. Let's go have fun for a few minutes then we'll get back to work."

"Okay." This time she met his hand halfway when he reached for hers and tried not to overanalyze how amazing it felt to simply hold his hand.

Chrissie had never seen such a huge area of bubbles before.

Agnes had set up a special non-slip floor and then had machines create mountains of bubbles. Currently, hundreds, maybe thousands, of children and adults alike danced and played in the bubbles to the directions of the emcee in a bubble-a-thon fund-raiser.

"Put your right hand in. Put your right hand out," he instructed.

"You have extra clothes?"

Her head jerked toward Trace. "What?"

"Did you bring extra clothes?" he repeated, taking off his tennis shoes and raising her feet one at a time to do the same to hers.

"I'm a prepared kind of girl, but stop that," she demanded, attempting to pull her foot free and instead just helping him accomplish his goal. "I'm not going into—"

But he wasn't listening. He'd tugged her to the outskirts of the bubble floor and she was midchest-high in bubbles.

"Oh, my," she exclaimed, unable to resist lifting a handful of the foamy white stuff to her mouth and blowing it.

Joss would love this, she couldn't help but think.

"Put your left hand in. Put your left hand out," the emcee continued.

She wiggled her toes, letting the bubbles tickle her feet and bare legs beneath her shorts. A giggle escaped. A happy giggle. Oh, my. She didn't want to feel happy.

Chrissie frowned. What was she thinking? Of course, she wanted to feel happy. Besides, when was she going to have the opportunity to play in bubbles with hundreds of other people ever again?

Probably never.

This was fun. She was allowed to have fun.

"If we're going to do this, we're going to do it right," she informed Trace, holding her left hand out and shaking it.

"That was the plan." His grin was lethal and gave her more giddiness than the bubbles.

"I know what your plan is," she accused, trying to "splash" him, but the bubbles didn't cooperate, sticking to her hand instead and plopping back onto the sea surrounding them.

He laughed. With a wicked gleam in his eyes, he scooped up an armful of bubbles. "I'm not denying it."

"Which doesn't make it any better." Instinctively knowing what he was about to do, she took a few steps back, but only managed to plop down in the midst of the bubbles.

Laughing, he held out a hand and pulled her to her feet. She sputtered, clearing the bubbles from her face.

"You look good covered in bubbles." His eyes glittered with all sorts of mischief.

"Trace."

"What?" He gave her an innocent look. "You do. I like it."

Truthfully, she liked how he looked waist deep in bubbles, too. There were too many people around for her mind to go to romantic bubble baths, but seeing Trace laughing out loud had cracked something inside her.

Something that had been vital in protecting her from how she felt about him. How dared he break down her defenses with bubbles and laughter and talk of getting to know each other? Who did that?

Then again, nothing about Trace had ever been typical, so of course he'd use bubbles to knock down the barriers she'd erected between them. Bubbles.

No one could be standoffish when surrounded by bubbles.

"Shake your leg and be quiet," she ordered, but was unable to keep the smile from her face.

Maybe it was her inner child coming out. Maybe it was all the happy laughter around her. Maybe it was the happy gleam in Trace's eyes as he stood in bubbles. Maybe it was feeling alive and desirable and amazing because she was his focus. Maybe it was all of the above.

Regardless, she laughed and played along with whatever the emcee had going. They hokey-pokeyed through the rest of the song, then participated in a couple of the other bubble games.

When the emcee announced a bubble-snowman-building contest for kids ten and under, they made their way out.

"Admit it, you had fun."

"I had fun." No point in denying it. She was still smiling.

A teenaged boy came up and handed Trace two towels. Chrissie glanced around, amazed by the boy's appearance since towels weren't provided and they should have brought their own.

"Why did he bring us these?"

He waggled his brows. "I'm a resourceful man."

"Apparently," she agreed, taking the towel from him, and wiping off the bubbles clinging to her skin and clothes. "We weren't dressed for this."

"We were fine," he countered. "Most everyone is wearing T-shirts and shorts, except for the kids."

"Thank you."

His smile was amazing. Brilliant. Beautiful.

"You're welcome, Chrissie. Making you smile is my pleasure."

There were a dozen or so people on the medical crew. More than they'd needed tonight, but that would change with sun-up.

There were a few two-man tents at the back of the medical area so there would be medical staff close in case middle-of-the-night care was needed. Chrissie was rooming with one of the nurse-practitioner volunteers, a pretty woman in her late forties who worked with a local children's hospital and said she'd been volunteering with CCPO for the past couple of years, after one of her patients' family had mentioned how the organization had helped with expenses.

Chrissie liked hearing how the organization was

making a difference out in the real world, rather than just through the testimonies given on stage at the event. Somehow, hearing Bernadette say CCPO had helped one of her patients made it all so much more real.

She and Trace had checked to make sure the medical area was still slow, then she'd slipped off to her tent to grab her toiletries where she bumped into her roommate.

"I'm headed to the shower truck to wash the bubbles off myself," she told the smiling woman.

"I'll be heading that way before the rush, too," Bernadette said, from where she sat on her sleeping bag, holding her phone. "I'm going to call home and check on my husband and kids since there's not a need in the medical tent right now."

Chrissie nodded, then left their tent to give the woman a semblance of privacy. In reality, there was very little. Yet, four years ago, she and Trace had found ways to be alone, especially at night when they'd been the two manning the slow, midnight hours.

Trace.

She'd essentially agreed to get to know him.

Ha. What did that even mean? She wasn't sure.

At least he'd been upfront that his main goal was to sleep with her again.

What a goal.

What a man.

She hung her head and took a deep breath. Why was she even fighting him?

He was right. She wanted him as much as he wanted her.

Probably more.

But she was four years older, four years wiser, four years more mature. She didn't have wild sexual flings.

Especially premeditated ones.

Then again, trying to convince herself of greater maturity right after playing in a sea of bubbles probably wasn't the most effective argument she'd ever waged.

But, oh, how she'd had fun playing with Trace.

Who'd have ever thought she'd be surrounded by bubbles, dancing and acting goofy with Trace Stevens?

She'd have bet against those odds every time.

But she didn't regret it. How could she when she'd laughed more than she recalled laughing in months? Years?

No, that wasn't true. She laughed with Joss. Lots and lots. Goodness, but that kid made her happy.

And Savannah. Spending time with her best friend and her baby daughter made Chrissie happy, too. Prior to Savannah's wedding, her friend had stayed the night and they'd giggled the night away while Joss slept.

But it was a different kind of laughter, a different kind of happy, than she felt at the moment. She couldn't explain the difference, just recognized that there was one.

Maybe it had to do with how Trace had laughed along with her, that they'd shared some magical, fun moment.

Maybe, she tried to convince herself as she made it to the bath area.

Most of the CCPO participants were still at the bubble-a-thon. There wasn't a line at the shower trucks.

Chrissie quickly squeezed into one of the tiny stalls inside the eighteen-wheeler shower trailer, rented for the event, and stripped off her sticky clothes. She let the warm water sluice over her body, then shampooed her hair, suds trickling down her nakedness.

Her mind couldn't help where it went.

Not after seeing Trace again. Not after their bizarre conversation. Not after his telling her she looked good covered in bubbles.

He'd kissed her.

She'd let him.

Craziness.

How could she have pushed him away when for the first time in four years she'd felt physical excitement? When for the first time in four years her heart had sped up at a man's touch? When her whole body had zinged with awareness? When her thighs had squeezed with excitement?

She'd wanted to kiss him back. To really kiss him back. To drag him somewhere where they were less likely to get interrupted and kiss him until they'd both been breathless.

She wanted him now, in this tiny shower stall with her, and for the bubbles and warm water to be their only covering.

She leaned her head against the wall, letting the water rinse the suds from her hair and body.

Just remembering his kiss, letting her mind go beyond that kiss to previous kisses from four years ago, had her ribcage contracting around her lungs, making her breathing labored.

She finished showering, dried off the best she could in the tiny space, slipped on fresh clothes, then headed out of the truck and over to the sink area.

She got her teeth brushed, then headed back toward the path that would take her to Medical.

"Am I seriously lucky enough to bump into you here?"

She turned slowly, her gaze colliding with Trace's. "Guess that depends on what you call lucky."

"Any time I have the privilege of setting eyes on you."

Feeling vulnerable to the emotions fizzing through her, she frowned at him in hopes of at least having a moment to catch her breath. She'd thought she'd have longer before facing him again. "I don't recall you using cheesy lines four years ago."

Her frown didn't deter him in the slightest and his grin was potent.

"Telling the truth is not a cheesy line."

"Still, I don't recall you saying such things."

That seemed to break through whatever was making him smile so intently. "If I failed to tell you how lucky I felt four years ago then I did you a grave injustice. I felt very privileged that you noticed me."

"You were hard not to notice," she admitted.

"Because I kept finding reasons to bump into you? To ask you a question? To hand you something so I could touch you? I couldn't believe my luck in meeting you that weekend."

"I wasn't complaining." She hadn't. She'd been just as attracted to him and she hadn't tried to hide it. Not then. She might as well not bother now because she was failing miserably. The hot look in his eyes warned of that.

"Do you remember that first kiss, Chrissie?" His voice had lowered even though there was no one else on the path.

"Remind me," she said to be contrary, because she knew every ounce of attraction she felt for this man was shining from her eyes like a homing beacon.

"Everyone had gone to dinner. It was just you and me in the medical tent."

"We'd stayed to clean up from a suture one of the docs had done on a woman who had sliced her arm while opening a can in the kitchen," she added.

"But the moment we were truly alone for the first time, we came together like two magnets."

"We kissed," she corrected. They hadn't "come together like magnets" until much later that night. Which had quite blown her away. She'd never done anything like that before. Never.

"We're alone right now," he pointed out. "I could remind you with more than words."

"Someone could come along."

"I'm not sure I like this older, more practical version of you," he teased.

She was older, more practical. She had to be. Did that make her boring? She bit the inside of her lip. "I'm not the same woman I was four years ago."

"Neither of us are the same as we were four years ago."

Something in his voice said life had thrown a lot of things at him during that time.

"But I am attracted to you," she heard herself say.

His smile returned. "And?"

"Apparently, we share very potent sexual chemistry."

"Is that something you encounter often?"

She almost said, *Only with you,* but caught

herself just in time. She was already vulnerable enough.

"Not that often," she improvised. "What about you?"

"Not since you."

Three little words that made her heart sing. Okay, so he wasn't saying he hadn't ever experienced such a strong attraction, but that no one since her had made him feel that way. A minor, silly, little thing, but his admission made her happy.

Funny, because not for a second did she doubt the truthfulness of his words. She never had. There was something about him that she instinctively trusted, rightly or wrongly.

"You got quiet," he accused softly.

She nodded. "We're standing in the middle of a path between the bath area and the medical area. Maybe we should head back."

He nodded and stayed in step beside her. "Agnes said this is the first year you've been back to volunteer since we met. What kept you away?"

"It wasn't fear of running into you, if that's what you're thinking."

"Don't jump to conclusions, Chrissie."

"You're right. I just didn't want you to make assumptions that…"

"Where you are concerned, I'm doing my best not to make any assumptions. Not even the ones

I want to make. So, what kept you away? Family? Work?"

"Family."

"Tell me about your family."

Not likely, but she smiled and suggested, "Then you'll tell me about yours because that's all part of us getting to know each other?"

His nose wrinkled. "Okay, so you have a point. Let's talk about something besides family. Do you still live and work in Chattanooga?"

"Yes, I love my job at the hospital."

"You're a CVICU nurse, right?"

Pleased that he remembered, she answered, "Yes, I work in the cardiovascular intensive care unit." She straightened her shoulders proudly. "I was promoted to nurse supervisor a few years ago."

"That's great." He smiled. "I'd say your family must be proud, but that would take us full circle. So, I'm going to say how proud you must be of that accomplishment."

"I love taking care of patients and I always try to do my best. This time, hard work paid off."

"Have there been times in the past where it hasn't?"

She shook her head. "I didn't mean my comment that way. What about you? Tell me about working for DAW."

The medical tent was within sight and their steps had slowed.

"What do you want to know?"

"What made you decide you wanted to do that?"

"Probably Agnes and Bud's influence over the years. I wanted to make a difference. A buddy of mine had joined and convinced me that doing the same would give me a sense of accomplishment that I wasn't finding in Atlanta."

"Was he right?"

CHAPTER FIVE

GOOD QUESTION. BUT not one Trace could easily answer.

In some ways, joining had filled a need within him that had been gaping since Kerry died. In others, he now had holes where they hadn't previously existed.

Maybe life was one big trade-off after another.

"I'd do it again, so I guess that's a yes," he finally said, realizing they'd completely stopped moving. "I thought of you."

Surprise lightened the green of her eyes. "What did you think about me?"

"You know what I thought."

Her eyes rolled a little. "That we share a strong sexual chemistry?"

"Among other things."

Why he was telling her so much, he wasn't sure; it was just that he felt it imperative to be upfront with her, that anything else seemed inadequate.

"I'd never met anyone like you, Chrissie."

Her chest lifted a little, as if his admission had caused her to have to take a deep breath. "And now?"

Her question caught him off guard.

"What about now?"

She looked up at him with a fierceness that defied her petite size. "I'm trying to figure out exactly what you're doing, Trace. You've admitted your goal is to sleep with me again. Is that the ultimate goal or do you want more from me than this weekend?"

More questions that made him uncomfortable, but at least he had answers for these. Not answers written in stone, but answers nonetheless.

"I'll be back overseas soon, Chrissie. To pretend otherwise would be wrong. Anything between us would only be for the weekend."

Taking a deep breath, she nodded, as if she'd been expecting that to be his answer.

"Is that nod an agreement?"

"No, Trace, I'm not agreeing to those terms. I didn't come here looking for you, or for an affair, or for anything other than to volunteer. Despite what four years ago might have led you to believe, I don't have affairs just because one is on offer and would feel good."

"Maybe you should."

Trace's words haunted Chrissie as she tossed back and forth in her sleeping bag. She'd not gone to her tent until almost midnight, but that hour had struck long ago and her mind still raced too much for sleep to take hold.

This was ridiculous.

She needed sleep. Needed to get rest before tomorrow when they'd likely be busy all day with dehydration, heatstroke and minor injuries.

But no matter how long she lay there, sleep just wasn't going to happen. She should see if whoever was working the medical tent needed help, or maybe a few hours of shut-eye while she sat up.

Taking care not to disturb Bernadette, she climbed out of her sleeping bag and slipped from the tent. There was a three-quarter moon that lit the night sky so she could easily make her way through the few small tents that were close to the medical tent.

Quietly, she entered Medical and wasn't surprised by who she saw sitting at a table, reading one of the medical thrillers she'd donated.

"Chrissie?" He stood, stretched his lean body.

"It's not what you think," she began, but maybe it was, because she'd known he'd be in the tent. Hadn't she been drawn there like a moth to a flame because of that knowledge?

"What am I thinking?" His words were soft, slow, but his eyes danced with mischief.

"I couldn't sleep and thought I'd see if whoever was working needed help." Right. She doubted she was convincing him any more than she was convincing herself. She'd come to find him.

"It's been slow. Not a single person seeking care since before you left."

She nodded, took a deep breath, and glanced around the empty tent. "I'm wide awake. You want to grab a nap? I can wake you if someone comes in."

He shook his head. "I'm good." He studied her. "Why couldn't you sleep?"

Worried he could see right through her, she shrugged and sank into the chair across from where he'd been sitting.

"Me?" he guessed.

"Probably."

"I'm sorry if I'm causing you stress."

He didn't sound sorry. He sounded pleased at her admission. Then again, he hadn't made any pretenses about his interest. Quite the opposite.

"Is there something I can do to help?" he offered, causing her to look up and meet his gaze. He lowered into the chair across from hers.

"Are you promising you'd do it?" she countered, wondering how it was possible for him to be so attractive when she knew better. She did know better. But she was there all the same.

This time he was the one who shrugged. "Depends on what you say."

Okay, so the reality was that she knew it had been him in the medical tent and that he was most likely alone. Had that been the real reason she hadn't been able to sleep?

No, the real reason she couldn't sleep was that she'd been sexually frustrated for four years.

Four years.

The cure was right in front of her. Willing and eager.

She was an idiot for coming there.

She'd have been a bigger fool if she hadn't.

"I want you, Trace."

The amusement in his eyes darkened to desire. He swallowed, slowly, and with exaggerated motion in his throat.

"Chrissie." Her name came out a bit strained.

"You don't have to say anything or do anything, but I needed to say that. I needed to tell you, because no matter how much I may think I am strong enough to fight the attraction between us, I'm not."

He leaned forward, his gaze not wavering from hers. "You're okay with us being together this weekend?"

Okay with it? Ha. No, her brain wasn't. Not really. But her body, yeah, her body would never let her live it down if she ignored what a weekend with Trace offered. But this time, they'd have to be more careful. Not that they weren't last time, but Joss had arrived nine months later all the same.

Joss.

For a moment, she considered fleeing the tent, then realized how ridiculous she was being. She was a grown woman. A grown independent woman. If she wanted to have sex with a gorgeous man who had a history of making her feel amazing, then why wouldn't she embrace the opportunity?

"Yes." A huge weight lifted off her shoulder at the admission. "I'm sorry I protested so much. Seeing you again and feeling attracted to you caught me off guard."

Rather than looking triumphant, his expression was thoughtful.

"You're sure about this, Chrissie? You understand I'm not offering anything more than this weekend?"

She nodded. She understood quite well.

"I don't want anything more than this weekend." For the second time in her life, she was going to let go and experience a no-strings weekend with Trace.

"Chrissie." His hands flat against the table, he leaned forward. "You make me want to forget this whole event and sweep you to a hotel where I can have you to myself all weekend."

"We can't leave. Agnes and Bud need us." Not that his words didn't tempt. They did. But she wouldn't walk away from pulling the load she'd committed to.

"I know we can't," he agreed. "And I wouldn't leave, but you make me wish we could be alone in a comfortable bed in a comfortable room, with room service available twenty-four-seven so we could take advantage of every single moment."

She closed her eyes and imagined being locked away for a weekend with Trace, a weekend where they had nothing more to do than to pleasure each other. A weekend that didn't require more than throwing on a bathrobe to let room service in to deliver sustenance to keep up their energy. A weekend where she had Trace to herself and the rest of the world didn't exist.

Oh, my.

"So, now what?" she asked, knowing she had to get her imagination under control or she'd be jerking him across the table and demanding some of that attention right this moment.

He laughed. "I take you behind that barely private partition to my semi-comfortable cot and hopefully have my wicked way with you."

Chrissie swallowed. "Okay."

Okay. She couldn't believe she was saying okay. That she was agreeing to going behind a partition with Trace so they could get naked. No, they wouldn't get naked. They'd satisfy their needs as quietly and stealthily as possible.

That hotel room sounded more and more tempting.

"I know." He didn't clarify what he meant. He didn't have to. He was thinking the same thing she was.

Trace pushed away from the table, stood, and made his way to where she sat. He reached for her hand.

Just as she slid her hand into his, felt the tingles of awareness only he seemed capable of eliciting from her nerve endings, a noise at the entrance of the tent as someone pushed the flap open had them both looking that way.

"Hello?" a female voice called by way of greeting.

"Hi," Chrissie greeted the woman and little girl coming into the tent as she stood. Disappointment filled her that she and Trace had lost their privacy, but as she looked at the little girl her disappointment quickly turned into concern.

Trace moved forward and stooped to the little girl's level. "I'd ask what was going on, but I can tell. Does that rash itch as much as it looks like it does?"

The child nodded and scratched at her neck to prove her point.

"Sorry," the girl's mother said. "I know it's late." She gave her daughter a worried glance. "She didn't break out until we lay down. I feel guilty for bothering you so late, but she keeps getting worse and I was afraid to wait until morning."

"It's okay. That's what we're here for," Trace assured. "Come to the exam area where I can get a better look."

He flipped a switch on a propane-gas-powered light, causing that area of the tent to brighten significantly so he would be able to examine his patient more efficiently.

"It's driving me crazy," the little girl said, scratching her arms. "I itch and itch and itch."

"Don't scratch," her mother reminded her.

"But it itches," the girl said matter-of-factly.

"It will only itch worse if you keep scratching it," the mother told her as she lifted the child onto the table. "Let's let the doctor take a look so he can make you feel better."

"Hi, I'm Chrissie," she introduced herself. "I need you to fill out a couple of forms while Dr. Stevens checks your daughter and figures out what we need to do about this rash."

The woman nodded and took the clipboard Chrissie offered. After glancing over the papers, she began writing her responses to the standard questions.

"What's your name?" Trace asked the little girl, who was rubbing her arms up and down in an attempt not to scratch.

"Chloe."

"That's a pretty name. My cousin just had a little girl and she named her Chloe Jane."

"I'm Chloe Darlington." The girl rubbed more briskly.

"How old are you, Chloe?"

"Four."

Trace did a quick ENT examination, glad to see all normal findings rather than swollen tissue that might block an airway. Then he checked the little girl's rash more closely. Large, raised pruritic wheals with a pattern that only appeared on areas not covered by her clothing.

"Chloe, have you ever had a rash like this before?"

The little girl shook her head.

"She hasn't," her mother confirmed, glancing up from the form.

"Hmm. This is an allergic rash, something we call a contact dermatitis, meaning that Chloe is allergic to something that she's come into contact with today."

"She didn't start breaking out until we got to our tent tonight. She was fine until then."

"Have you used any new products today?"

"Not that we know of." The woman thought a moment. "Well, other than her sleeping bag. That's new to her as she's never camped before, but I've used it a few times in the past so it wasn't brand-new."

Trace looked at the pattern of the rash again. "What was she wearing in the sleeping bag?"

"She was in her T-shirt and panties."

Which matched the rash being on her legs, forearms, and not on her trunk.

"She's allergic to something in your sleeping bag."

"It's just a thin sleeping bag, not a down-lined one or anything. I have one of those, but was afraid she'd burn up in this heat," the woman rambled, thought a moment, and then got an *aha!* look on her face. "I treated all our bags with bug spray to repel mosquitoes and such. You hear about all these diseases and viruses and I wanted to try to prevent everything I could." She winced. "I sprayed it heavy."

Trace nodded. "I'm going to give her some liquid diphenhydramine. I think that will help. If we don't see any improvement fairly quickly, then I can administer some steroids intramuscularly, but I'd rather not do that if possible."

"So, we'll need to stay here for a while?" the little girl asked. "'Cause I'm tired." She yawned to emphasize her point.

Trace laughed. "Tell you what, once your rash calms down a little, which I believe it will with the medication, I'll let you and your mom take my cot because we can't put you back in your tent, and I'm going to want to be close in case you have further problems."

"You don't have to do that," the girl's mother assured him, looking embarrassed. "We don't want to be a bother."

"It's not a bother. I wasn't planning to sleep other than catnaps, anyway."

While overseas, in war-torn countries, there had been way too many nights he'd not slept more than in short snatches, while keeping on alert for danger to him and his patients.

Besides, he and Chrissie hadn't been planning to sleep.

Far, far from it.

CHAPTER SIX

"I'M GLAD SHE'S feeling better this morning," Trace told Linda Darlington as Chloe ran around the medical tent meowing happily as she pretended to be a cat.

"Me, too," the woman agreed, laughing softly as she watched her daughter. "Too bad I don't have her energy or resilience, because I sure didn't sleep enough last night to prepare me for today's activities."

The woman hadn't slept more than a few hours at most. Probably about the same as Trace. Because he'd given them his cot, he'd stretched out in a chair and caught a few hours of zees during the early morning hours. But, unlike the tired mother, he felt refreshed, excited to face the day.

Hopefully, Chrissie was the same. He'd insisted she return to her tent and rest. She was going to need it.

He had plans for her.

Plans he'd dreamed about during the short bit of shut-eye he'd gotten. Dreams in which it hadn't mattered where they were. He'd ravished Chrissie.

The way he'd wanted to ravish her last night.

The way he would have ravished her had they not been interrupted.

Would she feel the same about him, about them,

this morning? Or would she have second thoughts in the light of day?

"Youth is wasted on the young," the mother continued, interrupting his meanderings. "What about you? Do you have children?"

Trace shook his head. His life wasn't conducive to having children. It never would be. "Kids aren't my thing."

"Too bad. You're really good with Chloe. She told me this morning that you were her new boyfriend."

Trace laughed. "She only likes me because I made the itching stop."

"Perhaps," the woman said, smiling. "But I think it was more than that. You're all she's talked about since she woke up. That, and how she misses Freckles, her cat."

"Yeah, well, I'd see to it that she spends the night with Freckles and not in your tent tonight," Trace offered, glancing up to see Chrissie enter the tent, two plastic cups of steaming coffee in her hands.

"How's Chloe this morning?" she asked Linda at the same time as she handed one of the cups to Trace.

"All better." The woman beamed. "I was just telling Dr. Stevens how much we appreciate him. You, too. Y'all were great with Chloe last night. Thank you."

"No problem. Dr. Stevens here did all the work."

"What work? The wash-down and diphenhydramine you gave her did the trick." Trace glanced down at the coffee and noticed it was exactly the right color. Strong and black. Just the way he liked it. Did she recall that from before? "Thanks for this."

"You're welcome. You should probably go to the food tent before it gets busy. Ms. Perez is there, foot propped up, and is handing out napkins to people as they trickle their way through line. She's all smiles, despite the fact her ankle looks as if it was mauled."

He grinned. "I didn't think she'd leave."

"I'm glad she didn't. She was absolutely glowing as she greeted folks. She's a burst of sunshine first thing this morning."

"A morning person, like my Chloe, eh?" Linda said, motioning for the little girl to join them. "Speaking of breakfast, I'm going to take this one and head that way, too. Her dad and sister are headed that way. Thank you both, again."

"You're welcome. I'm glad to see she's back to normal."

The little girl meowed, then smiled.

Trace scratched his head. "Almost normal—I think her medicine transformed her into a cat."

Loving his comment, the little girl meowed a bunch more, making them all laugh.

"Come on, kitty. Let's go find you something to eat," her mother said, taking her hand. "Thanks, again."

"Cute kid. Makes me think of..." Chrissie's voice trailed off and rather than finish she took another sip of her coffee.

"Of?" he prompted, curious about her family. Did she have nieces and nephews? Cousins? He really knew nothing about her other than that she was a CVICU nurse who worked in Chattanooga. Did she come from a big family? A little family?

But rather than elaborate, she smiled and asked, "Were you able to get any sleep?"

"Some."

"But not much?"

"More than enough. Do I look that bad this morning?"

She ran her gaze over him and Trace fought the urge to straighten his shoulders and suck in his non-existent gut.

He was wearing what he'd put on after his shower the night before: a clean CCPO T-shirt and a pair of khaki cargo shorts. Although he'd shaved the previous night, he didn't need to run his hand over his jaw to know he'd find a light growth of stubble there.

"Not that bad," she finally said, lifting her gaze to his, mischief dancing in the green depths. "But I've seen you better."

The corners of his mouth tugged upward. If she had regrets about what she'd said the night before, she wasn't showing them. Instead, she was outright flirting with him and he wanted to puff out his chest like a prized rooster.

"Maybe later we can talk about you seeing me better again."

She smiled a little smile that spoke volumes. "Who needs to talk?"

Oh, Chrissie, he thought as his body responded to her flirty grin and comment.

"Who indeed?"

Talking certainly wasn't what was on his mind while he took in the petite blonde woman in her mid-thigh-length shorts and CCPO medical staff T-shirt that fit her curves just right.

The rest of the medical crew had joined them in the tent and two of the members were rolling up the sides to the tent so they could see out, while another had flipped on a large commercial-grade fan to circulate air through the tent.

Outside, the event campgrounds were coming to life as volunteers and participants made their way toward the main tents. Everything would officially kick off for the day at seven. Once things got rolling, so would minor injuries.

"Do you want to come with me to grab a bite?" he asked, despite the fact that she'd already been to the food tent.

She shook her head and held out her coffee cup. "I've eaten and this will hold me over until later. I'm going to go man my triage station. I'll see you when you get back."

"Definitely," he promised. She'd be seeing him as much as he could arrange this weekend.

Beyond that, who knew? Maybe he'd suggest spending as much time together as possible before he headed back overseas.

Flirting with Trace was fun. And easier than it should be, Chrissie thought later that afternoon.

Had someone told her just twenty-four hours ago that she'd be catching Trace's eye and winking at him, she'd have told them they were certifiable. But she and Trace had some serious sparks flying back and forth between them.

Sparks that were bubbly and exciting and made her feel gloriously feminine.

Not just feminine…sexy.

Sexy.

Something she'd not felt in far too long.

Her days and nights were filled with being a good nurse and a great mother. She was content with her life. Better than content. She was happy and felt blessed.

But Savannah was right. There had been something missing. That feeling one got when an attractive man looked at you and his want was so palpable that desire itself caressed you.

That feeling one got when in the new bud of a relationship, when everything was exciting and new.

Only none of this was new. She wasn't in the

bud of a relationship with Trace. Whatever happened this weekend was it. They both knew that.

So, why did she still feel so giddy?

She wasn't the kind of woman to have random affairs. Or to have affairs, period.

She was giddy. Giggly giddy, even.

And not just because Trace couldn't seem to go more than a few minutes without stealing a glance her way or finding some reason to come talk to her in between the fairly steady stream of patients who came to the tent.

"He's a good man."

Chrissie blinked up at Alexis. Somehow the doctor still managed to look exotically glamorous in her dark shorts and CCPO medical staff T-shirt. How was that even possible? "Pardon?"

"Trace. He's a good man."

"You know him well?" she couldn't keep from asking despite the fact Trace had already said he hadn't slept with the woman. Was she seeking confirmation of what he'd told her?

No, she believed him. As he'd said, he had no reason to lie to her and he hadn't made any false promises.

"Not as well as I'd have once liked, as I suspect you know."

Chrissie couldn't prevent her blush.

"I'll admit that when I heard he was going to be here, I'd hoped to kindle a spark. The moment I saw the way he looked at you I knew that wasn't going to happen." She didn't bother to hide her disappointment. "So, despite a momentary surge of jealousy, I find myself happy for him, because he really is a good guy."

With the woman's blunt honesty, it was difficult not to like her.

"How does he look at me?"

Sliding into the chair across from the triage table, Alexis laughed.

"Like he wants to gobble you up and lick the crumbs from his fingers." She air-kissed her fingertips with great show. "The way I wished he looked at me."

There went the heat in Chrissie's cheeks again.

"So, are you going to tell me about you two?"

More heated cheeks.

"I like him, if that's what you mean."

Alexis rolled her dark, heavily fringed eyes. "Tell me something I don't know."

Although she owed Alexis no explanation, she found herself wanting to talk to the woman. Probably because Alexis had worked with Trace outside this sheltered tented event world and knew a side of him that Chrissie had never seen.

"We met four years ago at this event," she said. "I haven't seen or heard from him since. If anything, he's only gotten sexier with age, and I'm not blind."

"Neither is he. I've never known him to be so taken with someone."

"He didn't date when y'all worked together?"

"Oh, he dated, but I never saw him look at any of them, or me, the way he looks at you."

"That's…" she searched for the right word "…nice."

Alexis laughed again. "Nice? Honey, nice has nothing to do with it. Hot. Now, there's a better description. You're a lucky girl."

"You've no idea," she said, thinking of Joss. Which gave her a huge twinge of guilt. Alexis was telling her what a great man Joss's father was. How could she justify not telling him about their son?

Because memories of her own father snatching her away from her mother caused her insides to clam up with fear?

Trace wasn't her father. She knew that. But…

"You're right," the woman admitted. "I don't have any idea. Trace and I went out a few times, but I was more interested than he was. Like I said, you're a lucky girl."

Alexis confirmed what Trace had said. He hadn't slept with the beauty-queen doctor. She hadn't doubted him, but hearing the confirmation made her like Alexis all the more. Made her that much more giddy about Trace's interest.

"So tell me about you until the next patient comes in for me to see. Or we can send them Trace's way and continue with our girl talk," Alexis suggested with a wide smile that flashed her toothpaste-ad teeth again.

Pushing aside the nagging guilt her heart felt over not telling Trace about Joss, and giving in to her brain's reminder that just that morning she'd heard him say he didn't want children, Chrissie smiled and began telling Alexis about Chattanooga, her much-loved job at the hospital, her mother, and her friend Savannah.

She was surprised by how much she liked Alexis and that she could easily see herself becoming good friends with the forthright woman had they lived closer.

What in the world were Chrissie and Alexis laughing so hard at? Trace wondered as he made a quick note on the patient he'd just finished examining. The event wasn't keeping extensive medical records, but they were documenting each encounter and what was done.

Actually, to see the two women having a friendly conversation at all surprised Trace. So much for Chrissie's jealousy from yesterday.

Not that she'd had any reason to be jealous. He liked Alexis well enough. She was an intelligent, beautiful woman, but there just hadn't been any chemistry.

Chemistry wasn't a problem with Chrissie.

They had so much chemistry they could add new elements to the periodic table.

Another outburst of laughter had him sliding the paper he'd scribbled a few notes on into a manila file that would later be scanned into and stored on a computer.

Leaving his work area, he headed over to Triage. "You two are having way too much fun."

"Jealous?" Alexis asked, but not in a way he took as flirtatious, more as if she was teasing him because she'd figured out Chrissie majorly got to him.

"Absolutely. What does a man have to do to join in?"

"Just pull up a chair," Chrissie assured him, gesturing to an empty chair at a nearby table.

Trace didn't hesitate. He grabbed the chair and moved it to where the two women sat. "Now, tell me what's so funny, because I need something to make me laugh after that last blistered foot I treated."

Chrissie grimaced. "She looked like she was miserable when she hobbled in here. Is she going to be all right?"

"Yeah, but she's not going to be on her feet much for a few days. She's going to hang out on the sidelines in a chair and encourage the other participants."

"That's good," Chrissie said, her gaze locked with his and dancing with delight.

He smiled. He couldn't not smile. Which felt so damned good. Not so long ago he couldn't have brought a smile to his face had someone offered him the world.

Not since the hospital explosion in Yemen when friends had died because he'd not been able to save them.

Not since holding children ravished with starvation and disease while they died and promising himself he'd do all he could to save the next child, to bring medical care, food, supplies, into places where no sane person would venture.

Had he really deep down laughed since Kerry died?

Maybe he'd forgotten how to laugh.

Odd that a look from Chrissie could achieve that, could reach deep inside and bring forth a balm of peace and happiness.

"Well, as much as I enjoy watching the show, I'm going to leave you two alone for a bit and go grab a bottled water while we're in a lull. You want anything?" Alexis asked, cutting into his thoughts as she stood.

His gaze shifted. "I'm good. I've still got half a bottle from the last time one of the volunteers came by with drinks."

"Tsk. Tsk," Alexis scolded. "Make sure you hydrate well. Can't have you getting heatstroke on us." She turned her attention to Chrissie. "Lovely talking with you. Have fun and we'll catch up later."

"Thanks. I will." Chrissie smiled at the retreating woman. "I like her."

"I noticed. What did she mean by have fun?"

Chrissie shrugged. "You'd have to ask her."

"Despite the fact I'm convinced you know exactly what she meant?"

"Well, not exactly."

"But close?"

"Possibly."

Trace laughed. "Well, whatever she meant, I appreciate her giving us privacy. How's your day so far?"

"Not as busy as I recall us being four years ago," she admitted. "But steady for the most part."

"Not being as busy is a good thing. Hopefully it means people are taking precautions to prevent heat issues and injuries."

"I'm not complaining that we're not swamped," Chrissie assured him. "I want things to go well for the participants and volunteers. But I'm used to being busy. The gaps between patients can get tedious."

"Bite your tongue before you jinx us," he scolded.

"What? Afraid we'll have more late-night interruptions?"

"Alexis is 'manning the tent tonight,'" he reminded her. "George, one of the paramedics, volunteered to stay with her."

"I bet he did. She's a beautiful woman."

"So are you."

Her lashes lowered. "I wasn't fishing for a compliment."

"I didn't think you were, but you are a beautiful woman."

"Beauty is in the eye of the beholder."

"My eyes behold your beauty quite proficiently. As a matter of fact, I'd say they were experts at beholding your beauty."

She snorted. "I'd rather be appreciated for my brains."

"Seriously?"

She nodded.

"What is it about your brain you would like me to appreciate most? Your medulla oblongata? Your cerebellum? Your sulcus? A little gray matter, maybe?" he teased, loving the light shining over the darkness that seemed perpetually to permeate his inner being.

She wrinkled her nose at him. "I was thinking more along the lines of my brilliant conversation skills, my amazingly humorous wit, my—"

"Propensity for the truth?"

She laughed. "Exactly."

"You have all that and more. Brains and beauty."

"And you, Dr. Stevens, have the gift of the gab."

"Not really."

"No?" She arched a brow at him. "Because so far you've done a good job of talking me up."

"Is that what I'm doing?"

"Aren't you?"

He grinned. "I'm glad you changed your mind, Chrissie."

Red stained her cheeks and she glanced around the tent to make sure no one else could hear.

"Shh, I'd rather not advertise."

"No one knows what we're talking about, and if they did, so what? We're two consenting adults."

"True, but I'd just as soon not broadcast our personal business to the entire medical crew."

"I'll forewarn you that Bud and Agnes will take one look at us and know."

"You think?"

He nodded. "They knew we were involved four years ago. It won't be difficult to figure out that we've rekindled the fire."

She studied him. "Does that bother you?"

"I wasn't the one worried about someone overhearing our conversation," he reminded her, reaching out to brush his finger across her cheek as if he were wiping away a speck. He hadn't been. He'd just wanted to touch her, to feel her soft skin beneath his fingertip, to reassure himself that she was real.

"True, but…"

"It doesn't bother me if they know, Chrissie. They figured out long ago that I'm no saint."

After all, Kerry had died on his watch.

"I'm not so sure about that. So far, every time I've seen Agnes, she's sung your praises."

Taking a deep breath, he shrugged. "I pay her to do that."

"Sure you do."

A hobbling group of women made their way into the tent and Trace stood from the chair and went to meet them.

"Right this way, ladies. We'll get you triaged and taken care of."

CHAPTER SEVEN

UNFORTUNATELY ONE OF the male volunteers had spotted a wasp nest and taken it upon himself to knock it down.

Instead, the wasps had knocked him down and attempted to take several others along the way. In the end, three different people had gotten stung. Ethan Meadows, the man who'd stirred up the wasps to begin with, had sustained a significant number of stings and had several areas of fairly extensive swelling.

Chrissie had ice packs on the sting patients and Trace was keeping a close check on Ethan due to the number of sting sites he had.

The rest of the afternoon passed quickly and they had a rush of sore feet and minor musculo-skeletal issues right before time for the children's Olympic-style games started up.

Chrissie had learned that this was the first year they'd added the children's events. Bud and Agnes had made a decision to make the event more family friendly as CCPO was for children and they were hoping this would be a success.

Both of the event founders had been in and out of the tent, checking on the volunteers, and specifically, she got the impression they were checking on Trace.

As if they were worried about him.

A few hours later, the crew took turns sneaking off to the food tent to grab something to eat.

When Chrissie got ready to go, she did a quick visual search for Trace.

"One step ahead of you," he said from close behind her. "Let's grab something and get a quick nap afterward."

"A nap?" She eyed him suspiciously. "It would be suffocating in my tent right now. Plus, I have a roomie."

He waggled his brows. "Then you should go to my tent."

"Do you have a tent?"

He looked upward. "Do I have a tent? Now, what kind of a question is that to ask a man?"

"A realistic one."

He laughed. "Yes, I have a tent, Chrissie. It's near some trees so it does have a little shade, but still, it's probably near as hot as yours. Is that a problem?"

"No." She shook her head. "Not a problem."

"Good answer."

Chrissie wouldn't let herself question whether or not it was. She'd made her mind up that she was going to enjoy this weekend with Trace all she could. For this one weekend she'd be a normal, healthy, twenty-eight-year-old female with a sex drive, not responsible single-mom Chattanooga Chrissie.

Although thoughts of Joss, of telling Trace about Joss, kept sneaking in and Chrissie would guiltily shove them aside. She couldn't tell Trace about Joss. He didn't want to know. He was a good man, would feel responsible. He didn't want children or to be tied down.

What if he did and Joss had to go through the hell Chrissie had? What if Trace took him overseas to some God-forsaken place and she never saw her son again?

Shaking her irrational fears from her mind, Chrissie went to get into the line to collect food.

"We're not eating here," Trace informed her.

Biting her lip, she stared at him. "We're not?"

"Nope. Wait here."

He walked to where a woman greeted him with a huge smile, nodded, then reached behind the counter where she was working.

She brought up a backpack and handed it to Trace. She said something to him, but Chrissie couldn't make out her words. He laughed, nodded, then thanked the woman.

Trace grabbed a couple of bottled waters from a volunteer manning a large iced container of drinks, then took Chrissie's hand and led her down a path away from the food station.

"You up for an adventure?"

"In your hot tent?" she guessed, by far not opposed to the idea. She was quite in favor of getting hot and sweaty with Trace. But she was pretty sure they were headed in the opposite direction from Trace's tent. From everyone's tents.

"Nah." He shook his head. "I'm saving my tent for later."

His answer piqued her curiosity. He wasn't going to haul her to his tent first chance he got? Go figure. She'd admitted she wanted him and he was going to drag out the moment in torturous ways. If she didn't know better she might think it was because he didn't want her as much as she wanted him. She did know better. His desire was in his eyes every time their gazes locked.

Still, she was curious as to what he had up his sleeve. "Okay, take me on an adventure."

Truth was, every second with Trace was an adventure. Had been every second she'd ever been in his presence.

When he led her to a gas-powered, four-wheel-drive all-terrain vehicle, reached into his cargo-shorts pocket and pulled out a key, Chrissie couldn't hide her surprise.

"What are you doing?"

He grinned. "What does it look like I'm doing?"

"Where are we going?"

"I told you. On an adventure." He opened the backpack the food-station woman had given him and dropped the bottled waters into it. "You mind wearing that? I would, but I'd rather have you pressed against me without a bag with our lunch in between us. Plus, I don't think you'd be nearly as comfortable."

"Not a problem." She slid the straps over her shoulders, letting the bag hang against her back. It wasn't super heavy, despite being stuffed full.

He handed her a helmet that had been hanging from one of the handle bars. "I know it's hot, but I want to make sure I keep you safe while we're on our adventure. Helmet on. Can't have us being the ones needing use of the medical station."

Staring at the machine nervously, she took the helmet. "I've never ridden on one of these. I'm not sure I'm going to like it."

If her nerves at the mere thought of just climbing onto the four-wheeled machine were any indication, she was pretty sure she wouldn't.

"Sure you will. You're an adventurous kind of girl."

Ha, that was a joke and a half. Unless working and spending every other spare moment with her son qualified as adventurous. Although she loved the unknowns of her nursing job and Joss was full of life and kept her hopping, she didn't think many would qualify work and motherhood as making her an "adventurous' kind of girl.

"Not that adventurous."

In reality, she supposed many would consider her boring, but she didn't feel that way with Trace, nor was he looking at her as if he found her boring.

"Except with you," she added. "You bring out my adventurous spirit."

Putting on his helmet, he grinned. "Works for me."

"What?" she asked, sliding the helmet on and fiddling with the strap until she had it snapped into place and snug beneath her chin.

Too bad they didn't make full-body helmets. She'd feel safer.

"You only being adventurous with me." He checked her helmet, then climbed onto the ATV and patted the seat behind him. "Hop aboard my chariot."

She snickered, not budging from where she stood, staring at the machine. "Some chariot."

"Don't judge a chariot by its ugly green color. It'll get us where we're going."

"Which is?"

He just grinned and patted the seat again. "I'm more of a show kind of guy than a tell kind of guy."

"Yeah, I remember that about you, but it's a vague memory. I may need a reminder soon."

He laughed, but didn't even try to steal a kiss, which he easily could have. Although there were vehicles and several motor homes around the area, she didn't see a single person. Maybe she should steal a kiss. Maybe that would distract him from wanting to go anywhere on the four-wheeler.

But part of her wanted to know what he had planned.

A strong enough part that she took a deep breath and steeled herself for whatever the "adventure" brought her way.

Hoping she didn't make a fool of herself by being terrified of riding on the four-wheeler, because, seriously, she wasn't feeling brave at all, Chrissie climbed on behind him.

"Wrap your arms around me and hang on," he advised when she settled onto the vehicle.

Advice Chrissie had no problem taking. She slid her arms around his waist and locked her fingers together. Her body was pressed snugly against his as he turned a switch and the vehicle roared to life between her legs. Oh, my.

"Hang on," he told her again, and then they were off.

Chrissie closed her eyes and said a little prayer that she didn't cut off Trace's air supply by clinging onto him too tightly.

"You okay?" he called over the engine noise.

"Fine," she said, loosening her grip a fraction and forcing her eyelids apart to stare through the helmet's clear visor.

Okay, this wasn't so bad. Actually, the wind whipping at her body felt good. Not as good as the man she pressed up against, but not bad.

At first, Trace kept the vehicle fairly slow, as they were still in the outskirts of the event area, but soon, they'd left behind the tents and the few people they'd encountered and were making their way through a lightly wooded area.

When they drove free of the woods and came into a grassy field, Trace called over the roar of the engine, "You ready?"

She knew what he meant. He'd been so cautious through the event area, through the woods, that instinctively she'd relaxed. Trace wouldn't do anything stupid. He'd keep her safe.

"Yes!"

She was. Ready for whatever he wanted.

The intensity between them for the past twenty-four hours-plus, on top of having her body firmly pressed against his, had her oh, so ready. Add in the vibration of the vehicle and, yeah, she was ready.

More than ready.

Unable to resist, she splayed her hands across his belly, loving the flat planes beneath her fingertips. She fanned them upward, pressed herself tighter against him, flattening her breasts into his back, and almost groaned at the pleasure.

But before she could do more, he gunned the gas and they took off across the field in a smooth motion that spoke of an easy familiarity with riding ATVs, and maybe being acclimatized to having women try to seduce him.

Which, she supposed, was what she was doing.

Because she wanted him.

Pressing her helmet against his shoulder, she

held on tight as she adjusted to the increased speed. Within seconds, she lifted her head and let the wind whip against the exposed parts of her body.

Okay, this was one adventure she could seriously get used to.

Only she wasn't sure she'd feel nearly as comfortable, nearly as safe, with anyone other than Trace.

What was it about the man that made her feel safe?

Funny, she hadn't thought about him making her feel safe four years ago, but he had.

Safe to be herself.

Safe to express herself.

Safe to tell him what she wanted, show him what she wanted.

Safe to feel all the delicious things he did to her body and to give right back.

That was the difference between Trace and any other man she'd ever met. With Trace, she hadn't felt self-conscious or nervous, she'd just felt…alive.

Adventurous!

Just as she did this very moment.

Laughter bubbled out from between her lips.

She wasn't sure how long they rode, but soon they came to another wooded area, and Trace significantly slowed their pace as they made their way through the trees.

Within a few minutes they came to a stream and just when Chrissie braced herself for the splash sure to come as he drove right through the foot or so of moving water, he brought the ATV to a stop and killed the engine.

"Out of gas?" she teased as he undid his chin strap, and pulled the helmet from his head. He hung it on the handlebar by the strap, then climbed off the four-wheeler, and reached for her hand.

"I hope not. That would be a long walk back."

She let him help her off the ATV and undo her chin strap, pulling the helmet from her head.

Figuring her hair was a mess from the helmet, heat, and sweat, she ran her fingers through it while he hung up the helmet.

"Don't. You look beautiful."

"You sure you had your visor pulled down? I think you may have gotten bugs in your eyes during our ride."

He laughed. "Not hardly."

Removing a rolled-up blanket that had been strapped to the back of the ATV, Trace spread it out a few feet from the stream.

"This is beautiful," she told him, looking around. It really was. The area wasn't heavily wooded, but enough so that it made her feel as if she were in some private enchanted forest, especially with the few sprigs of purple flowers that grew around the grassy area where he had spread the blanket. "Are we going to be in trouble for being here?"

He shook his head.

"You're sure?"

"Yep. I know the owner."

Something in the way he answered had her asking, "Bud?"

He shook his head again. "No, my father."

His father? She glanced around the gorgeous scenery again, taking in the gurgling stream, the green trees, the thick, grassy areas, the blue sky peeking in around the leaves.

"It's a beautiful piece of property."

"Yeah, he bought it several years back with plans to modernize it into an upscale suburb and golf course, but hasn't done so yet."

"Why not?"

"Mostly, because Bud and Agnes need the section they use for the event. Still, there's several hundred more acres beyond what the event uses, so I guess he could develop and not affect the event."

Sunshine danced on the water and where it hit the ground beneath the leaf cover above.

"It would be a shame for this to be destroyed to make a subdivision," she mused.

"I agree. Can I have the bag, please?"

She removed the backpack and handed it to him.

"Have a seat and I'll serve you lunch."

"A picnic?" she asked, sitting down near him on the blanket.

He grinned. "Yes."

He pulled out two plastic-wrapped sandwiches, a couple bags of baby carrots, fruit, and the two bottled waters. "If you're a good girl and eat all your food, I have dessert for you."

She just bet he did and he looked pretty scrumptious. "Oh, really?"

Nodding, he reached back into the bag and removed a small bottle of hand sanitizer. Holding out the bottle, he squirted a generous dollop into her hand then another into his own.

"Thank you for doing this, but are you sure it's okay for us to be away from the medical station this long? I'll admit I'm feeling a little guilty."

He smiled a smile that said he understood and didn't judge her anxiety. "Alexis has my number and instructions to call if it gets busy. We could be back in twenty minutes tops."

Interesting.

"Alexis, huh? Was she in on this?"

"Not really. I just asked if she minded holding the fort down while I stole you away for a while. I think she approved."

"I like her more and more."

"She's okay," he conceded, not sounding overly concerned one way or the other as he dug around in the backpack.

"For a beautiful cardiologist who volunteers to help raise awareness and funds for children with cancer."

"Well, yeah, at least she has that going for her." His tone was teasing. He pulled out a zipper-closed plastic bag that had napkins, et cetera, in it. "Hungry?"

"Starved."

Something in the way she answered must have keyed him into what she was feeling because he paused from digging more items out of the backpack, and he glanced at her. "Yeah?"

She nodded.

He scratched his head. "What am I doing?"

She shrugged. "I don't know. What are you doing?"

"Not what I want to be doing."

She fought the urge to lick her lips because they definitely felt dry. "Which is?"

"Touching you."

No more suppressing her tongue after that comment. She moistened her lips.

"Well." She stared straight into his eyes. "Today is your lucky day because if you act now, you can touch me."

He arched a brow. "If I act later?"

"You can touch me, then, too."

Trace touched.

Just a light brush of his fingertip over her cheek that he continued down her throat, toying at her T-shirt collar.

But, oh, what a touch.

Despite the September heat, goose bumps prickled her skin and caused his to do the same.

She was looking at him. He could feel her gaze hot on his face, but his stayed in tune with the trail his finger was blazing; he was mesmerized by what his touch was doing to her flesh.

More than just his finger, because now he brushed his hand down her arm, light, feathery, surreal as the sun dappled on the ground around them, giving a magical feel as the wind blew, gently swaying the tree limbs above them and kissing their skin with the breeze.

Lower down her arm he moved until he touched her hand. He traced each finger, noting her short, clean nails. She wore no jewelry other than a pair of small diamond stud earrings, something he'd noticed four years ago, as well. He'd bet anything the earrings were the same ones she'd had on then, that she wore them continuously. Had they been a gift from someone? A family member or a former man in her life?

He laced their hands and lifted hers to press a kiss there.

"You know this isn't necessary, right?" Her voice was low in her throat, almost husky as their eyes met. "You don't have to seduce me or convince me to say yes. I'm yours for the taking."

He groaned. "I'm going to take you."

"Then get on with it."

He laughed at the full pout of her lips, but he'd be lying if he didn't admit, at least to himself, that her urgency thrilled him.

"What's your rush?" He slipped his hand beneath her T-shirt hem and lifted upward. With her help, he pulled the shirt over her head, revealing her peach-colored bra and creamy skin beneath.

He sucked in a breath at what he'd uncovered, then resumed his exploration by rubbing his hands over her bare shoulders, down her sides.

Rather than answer his question with words, Chrissie reached behind her, undid her bra, then slipped free of the material.

"There," she said, guiding his hand to cover her breast. "That's better."

She was right. That was better.

But not good enough.

He lowered and took her nipple into his mouth and sucked on the pebbled flesh. He'd already been hard. He'd been hard from the moment he'd touched her cheek, had been fighting an erection the entire ride over to his favorite spot along Horse Shoe Creek. Now, he was painfully so, but refused to rush this.

It had been four years since he'd kissed her, touched her, been inside her.

Four years too long.

He didn't want it to be over before he got started. Once inside her, he didn't think he was going to last long.

At least, not nearly long enough.

All night wouldn't be nearly long enough.

He planned to give her as much pleasure as

he could before giving in to the hedonistic need within him that just wanted to thrust deep inside her and possess her with all his might, to claim her body with his in the most elemental way.

Just the thought had him groaning against her full breast. He really liked the added roundness to her bosom, her hips, the new hourglass curves of her body.

Her fingers were in his hair now, threading through the locks and pulling him closer. She moaned and her arms slightly buckled beneath her as she arched toward him.

"Lie back," he ordered, gently pushing her against the blanket. There was a thick bed of grass and moss beneath them to serve as a cushion, but he wouldn't put his weight on her, not until he was ready to take her, just in case. He wanted her comfortable so nothing would distract from what he was doing.

"I'm going to take off your shorts, Chrissie."

Eyes closed, she nodded, but as his fingers slid beneath her waistband she slightly sat up and stopped him by grasping his head and pulling his mouth to hers.

She kissed him.

Not a gentle kiss, but a kiss full of hot need.

A kiss that demanded his very being.

A kiss that gave her complete control of him.

"Chrissie," he breathed the second their lips parted.

He helped her when she pulled off his shirt. He helped her when she undid his shorts and freed him to her greedy touch.

He almost lost it.

"Take your shorts off," he ordered as he slid out of his own, grabbing a condom from his pocket before he was too far gone to care. He almost already was.

He heard her gasp and winced. Hell. How could he have forgotten the jagged scar along his left lower abdomen?

"What happened?"

"Long story." He didn't want to talk about what had happened in Shiara right now. Not ever really.

She ran her finger over the puckered skin, but Trace was having no more of it. He didn't want her pity or whatever that was in her eyes. He wanted the passion from before she'd seen his damaged flesh. The passion that was still there and that he was determined to hold onto.

He ripped open the condom, had the prophylactic on in record speed, and rolled on top of her. "You're sure?"

Rolling her eyes at his question, she lifted her hips to where he nudged against her. "Please."

Making sure to support his weight, Trace pushed into her. Slow and steady at first, then faster, until he couldn't think, couldn't breathe, couldn't do anything but feel as the amazing heat between their bodies built, then combusted.

CHAPTER EIGHT

STILL TRYING TO catch her breath, Chrissie stretched to where she could kiss Trace.

Thank goodness she'd decided to take full advantage of him being close and wanting her.

The man was amazing. Simply and purely amazing.

He still felt amazing and full between her legs, almost to the point that she'd question whether or not he'd orgasmed. Almost.

She squeezed her inner thighs around him, eliciting a manly growl.

"Unless you're prepared for round two, I'd advise you not do that again, because, lady, you make me feel like Superman."

Although she was sweaty and breathy from round one, Chrissie gave him a look that hopefully left no doubt in his mind of what she wanted. She planned to take advantage of every second with him. With a saucy smile, she squeezed her thighs again and liked the light that instantly lit in his hot gaze.

Later, much later, she would question him on what had happened to his beautiful body.

The following morning, Chrissie stood on her tiptoes to the side of the main stage and listened to the farewell program with a heavy heart.

She cried out in release before he did, but just barely as he toppled over right behind, then collapsed.

"I forgot," she whispered against his throat, her arms wrapped tightly around him as she held him close. "I forgot how amazing sex was with you."

He propped himself up on his elbows and stared down at her, at the awe and joy in her sated eyes. Something shifted in his chest. He didn't know how to label it, just that she moved him in powerful ways.

"I didn't," he admitted, kissing the tip of her nose. "I've thought about you, this, a million times."

She had slept in Trace's tent with him the night before. They'd had to be quiet, to keep their movements and reactions under control, but they had made love. Twice.

She was a little sore today, but not so much that she didn't wonder if they'd get the opportunity to make love again, before she headed back to Chattanooga that afternoon.

Back to Joss. Trace's son.

She sucked in a breath and reminded herself the same thing she'd reminded herself of over and over during their night together. She wasn't going to go there.

Currently, Agnes was on the main stage giving a final speech and congratulations to all the participants and volunteers on the fabulous job they'd done. Between the previously obtained participant sponsors and the multiple weekend events, they'd raised seven figures to further their cause and Agnes couldn't be prouder.

Having worked the night before, Alexis had headed out that morning after exchanging numbers with Chrissie and promising that they would get together again at some point in the future.

Who knew if they really would, but it was a nice sentiment.

All that was left after Agnes's talk was the final farewell from Bud. Then the participants would head out. The remaining volunteers would pack up leftover supplies. Rented and donated equipment companies had already started arriving to collect their items. Perishables would be donated and anything they could use for the next event would be boxed up and labeled in plastic bins.

Trace and Chrissie planned to help break down the medical station, so they would get to spend a little more time together. But every second seemed like sand falling faster and faster through an hourglass that would separate them forever.

Because despite how wonderful the past twenty-four hours had been, no matter how wonderfully sweet and tender Trace had been that last time he'd made love to her just before dawn, she didn't fool herself that it was anything more than exactly what they'd agreed to.

A no-strings weekend affair.

In just a few hours, they'd say goodbye. She'd go home. He'd leave for parts unknown again or whatever it was he planned to do with the rest of his life.

The end.

She didn't regret their weekend.

Far from it.

Despite the nagging ache in her chest, she was grateful she'd been given the opportunity to get to know Trace better, that this time they'd talked during those long hours about things besides, "Oh, that feels so good!" Not what had happened to him to cause the scar, as he'd brushed off her questions each time she'd asked, but they had talked about a lot of things. She was grateful that if Joss ever asked about his father she could smile and tell him about a man she knew cared about others and made a difference in the world.

A man she wished Joss could know firsthand.

Not going there, she repeated over and over in her head. They'd agreed to a no-strings-attached weekend. He'd said he didn't want children four years ago and he'd repeated the sentiment to Chloe's mother. To tell him would be selfish.

Would be risky, the fear that lurked within her added.

"What are you thinking?"

She cut her gaze to the man occupying her thoughts and went for the truth. Mostly.

"That you and I will be saying goodbye in a few hours."

His expression tightened, then he seemed to make a quick decision. "We don't have to."

Her heart skipped a beat. What was he saying?

"You could stay in Atlanta tonight," he suggested, excitement glittering to life in his eyes. "I could take you somewhere nice for dinner and we could spend the evening together." His gaze searched hers. "The night."

Oh, how he tempted her.

But she'd only made arrangements with Savannah to keep Joss until this evening. Plus, she missed her little boy.

She needed to get back to Chattanooga, to her life there.

She looked into Trace's face and saw so much of her son there. Same eyes, same straight nose, same strong chin. Same stubborn determination.

What would he think if he knew they'd had a son together?

That they had a beautiful three-year-old little boy who was the spitting image of him? Would he want to know Joss? Would he care? Or would he take off for parts unknown without batting an eyelash?

What if he took Joss from her? Her father had never wanted her and he had still tried to take her. Not that Trace was anything like her father, but once upon a time her mother had believed in her father, too.

Panic filled Chrissie and she shook her head.

"No, we can't spend the night together?" he asked, misinterpreting her head shake.

She wasn't staying, wasn't going to call Savannah to beg for one more night. Her friend would say yes, but...

"I need to go home, Trace."

His disappointment was palpable. "Are you scheduled to work tomorrow?"

"Not until Tuesday, but—"

"But you need to go home to do laundry and wash your hair?"

His tone was so sarcastic and unlike anything

she'd heard come from his mouth that she was a little taken aback.

"I didn't say that, but I do need to go home."

His gaze was steely. "Why?"

"I have things I have to do, Trace. A life there that I've been away from all weekend."

"A life that can't wait one more day?"

She closed her eyes. She wanted to stay with him, wanted to let him bring her body over the top time and time again, but then she'd be faced with leaving tomorrow. Then, she'd be faced with explaining to Savannah why she needed another night, not that her friend wouldn't be understanding. Savannah would probably be the opposite and encourage her to go for it.

But every second she spent with Trace made her question more and more how he'd react if she told him about Joss.

Every smile, every touch, every laugh they shared made her crave to see him with their son, to hear and see the two of them interact, laugh, play.

Every time she considered telling Trace she battled guilt and the terror she'd faced as a child at the hands of her father.

She couldn't spend more time with Trace. She just couldn't.

"No, it can't." She braced herself for whatever his reaction might be, but when he spoke he sounded like his normal self again.

"We would have had a great time, Chrissie. I won't lie and say I'm not disappointed."

Sighing in relief, she reached for his hand. "We have had a great time. That I need to go home now doesn't change that."

Glancing at her, he considered what she said, then grinned. "You're right. We have had a great time. Thank you."

They finished listening to the event farewell then made their way back over to the medical station. They worked side by side, chatted, made a few jokes with the other volunteers who'd stayed to help, but the last few grains of sand quickly fell and soon it was time for Chrissie to go.

She didn't want to. She wanted to stay, to spend every single second that he'd give her for however long that might be. Silly. She'd already had more than she'd ever dreamed she would just in getting to see him again, to make love to him again.

She'd also learned so many things about him during the hours they'd lain in his sleeping bag talking.

He was an only child. He'd gone to private schools his whole life, including college, and medical school. His father had wanted him in the family business, but Trace had wanted to be a doctor, so he had become one. Bud and Agnes really were his godparents and he considered them the major influences on who he was. His mother had a good heart, but was a social butterfly who lived in the shadows of his father and was content there. Trace never had been. Both his parents were in good health and his grandparents had died of old age.

All things that were important to know about her son's father's family.

More guilt hit her.

Before this weekend, she'd never really considered tracking Trace down to tell him about Joss. Not more than in brief little snatches.

By the time she'd realized she was pregnant almost three months had gone by since she'd seen him. He hadn't contacted her. Not once. She'd had no reason to think he'd have wanted to know about their son. Quite the opposite, really.

She still didn't.

Just because they shared a dynamic chemistry didn't mean a thing except that they were highly sexually compatible.

That they most definitely were.

Ugh. She had to stop with this internal battle. There were compelling reasons why she wasn't going to tell Trace.

Chrissie said goodbye to the volunteers she'd met. Trace got hung up talking to one of them who was considering signing on with Doctors Around the World, and while they talked Chrissie went to track down Agnes and Bud to say her goodbyes. She found Agnes supervising the equipment-rental company breaking down the food service area.

"You headed out?" Agnes asked when she spotted Chrissie coming toward her.

"I am. I packed my things up into my car this morning and we just finished packing the supplies in the medical station."

Agnes stopped what she'd been doing, wiped her hands down the side of her shirt. "Hope we'll see you again next year."

Next year.

Would Trace be there or would he still be off in another country doing good for those in need?

She and Joss needed him.

The thought was silly, but it ran through her mind, causing her to wince.

No, she and Joss did not need him. She took great care of her little family.

"I'm not sure where I'll be next year, but maybe." She gave an answer because Agnes waited for one.

"Trace know you're about to leave?"

"He was helping the crew load up the heavy stuff, then got caught up talking about Doctors Around the World when I headed this way. I'll find him and say goodbye before I leave."

Although it would be better to just go.

"You two going to see each other again?"

She fought grimacing at Agnes's question. "No."

Disappointment marred Agnes's face and she gave a little shake of her head. "I hate to hear that. You're good for that boy."

Trace was hardly a boy, but Chrissie wasn't going to point that out.

"He was good for me, too."

The weekend had been good for her. As hard as the thought of saying goodbye to Trace was, she was glad she'd come to the event, glad she'd volunteered and been a part of something so wonderful to help others, glad she'd run into Trace and put the bitterness she held toward him to rest.

Hopefully for good.

Hopefully she'd go home and love their little boy and only think of Trace with fond memories of the man who'd given her life's most precious gift. Her son.

He'd been honest with her. He wanted nothing more than what they'd already shared. Well, that and one more night of hot, steamy sex in the comfort of a bed.

Funny, but she had a difficult time imagining anything being better than what they'd already shared on a blanket dappled in sunshine and a sleeping bag in the shadows.

Yeah, it was time to go because she was becoming an emotional mess.

She looked at Agnes and the woman saw right through her.

"You need to tell him."

Knowing what she was about to do, she shook her head. "It's better this way."

Agnes wasn't buying it. "Better for who?"

"Both of us."

"Are you married?"

"What?" she asked at Agnes's unexpected question.

"I'm just trying to imagine what reason there could be for you to walk away from Trace."

What about the facts that he'd be leaving to go overseas, that he didn't want a committed relationship, that he didn't want children? What about Chrissie's baggage that dogged her with the fear of him grabbing Joss and running, even when she logically knew Trace would never do such a thing?

What about the fact that Trace could so easily break her heart?

"I know you don't understand, Agnes, and for that I'm sorry, but I had no expectations and neither did Trace."

The older woman shook her head. "Young people these days."

Yeah, she supposed to Agnes it did seem that she probably did sleep around without another thought, but, even with as much as she liked Agnes, she didn't know the woman well enough to explain to her that wasn't the case.

Even if she did, that would raise too many other questions. Like why had she slept with Trace so quickly four years ago? Why had she set aside common sense and had sex with him repeatedly this weekend?

Because Trace was different.

He always had been.

What that difference was she couldn't allow herself to label, especially not while Agnes studied her with an expression that wavered from disappointed to sympathetic.

Yeah, if she allowed herself to really care about Trace she'd need sympathy, because she'd be facing even bigger heartache than she had the last time they'd said goodbye.

Good thing she'd gone into this knowing all they had was the weekend because falling for Trace would have been easy.

Which was why she hugged Agnes and said goodbye.

Goodbye to Agnes, to Atlanta, and to Trace.

"What do you mean she left?" Trace frowned at the woman he'd loved and admired his whole life.

Agnes had marched into the empty shell of the medical tent where he'd been talking to one of the volunteers and insisted upon speaking to him. He was grateful she'd waited until they'd left the medical tent to announce her news in private.

"You heard me," Agnes countered, her hands going onto her hips as she gave him a motherly stare-down. "Apparently, you didn't say or do the right things, because she told me bye and apparently already had her car packed, because she left."

Yeah, he'd helped her carry her things to her car that morning after they'd broken her tent down.

"I said and did the right things," Trace argued. He'd been upfront with her that time spent with him was only for the weekend.

It didn't matter that she'd just left without saying goodbye.

Not really.

She'd probably done them both a big favor, because he'd have tried to convince her to spend the night with him again.

She'd already said no so trying to persuade her further would have been pathetic on his part.

He wasn't a pathetic or desperate kind of guy.

At least, he never had been in the past.

These last four years hadn't presented him with much opportunity to date or have relationships with women. Sure, there had been a few female volunteers, but for the most part he'd been celibate and hadn't had any interest in dating.

Or in sex.

He'd blamed his lack of interest on the situations he'd been in. On the stress and the extreme conditions of the areas where he'd been working.

Maybe it had been more than that.

Maybe it had been memories of a certain woman.

"Well," Agnes interrupted his thoughts. "What are you going to do about her leaving?"

He blinked at his godmother and almost smiled at her feigned, or not so feigned, outrage. "Not one thing."

He wasn't. Although he wanted one more night, he could see the plus sides to her having left. Saying goodbye to Chrissie wouldn't have been easy. Odd, as he didn't recall having problems telling her goodbye four years ago. Then again, he'd been leaving that week for parts unknown so he'd been saying goodbye to pretty much everyone.

He'd be doing that again within a few weeks.

Agnes frowned. "You're not going to go after her?"

"She left without saying goodbye," he reminded her, shoving his hands into his cargo-shorts pockets and fiddling with his keys. "A woman doesn't do that if she wants a man to come after her."

"Sure, she does."

Maybe in some cases, but not theirs. He shook his head. "That's not the kind of relationship we have."

Agnes harrumphed. "Well, sex every four years doesn't seem to be a very normal kind of relationship, if you ask me."

Trace winced, but stood his ground. "I didn't."

He was not talking sex with Agnes. Nope. He wasn't going to do it no matter how well meant her intentions were.

"Don't give me that look or that attitude," she warned in her most motherly tone. More motherly than his own mother's usual tone for sure.

"I know you like her," Agnes continued, not backing down.

"I never said I didn't," he reminded her, knowing that to resist was futile. Agnes had always been able to read him and it wasn't as if he and Chrissie had tried to hide their attraction to each other. At least, not after she'd gotten past her initial hang-up.

"Then why would you let her walk away?" Agnes's question echoed what was running through his mind.

Crossing his arms, he considered the woman he'd adored all his life, then shrugged. "She was avoiding having to say goodbye. I understand that."

On some levels, he really did.

"Well, I'm glad you do, because I sure don't," Agnes huffed. "I think you should go after her and see what happens."

Trace laughed. What would be the point?

"I already know what would happen."

Agnes's salt-and-pepper brow arched. "What's that?"

"We'd say goodbye."

"You seem so sure." Her disappointment was palpable.

Trace let out a long breath. "Whether today, tomorrow, or next week, we'd have to say goodbye. I'm leaving and will be gone for months on end. Perhaps years. This way is best."

Chrissie was still telling herself that leaving was the best thing for her and Trace when she was at

Savannah's house that evening. The farther away she got from Atlanta, the more unsure she became.

Part of her knew she'd done the right thing.

A goodbye between her and Trace would have been messy. Just look at how messy their talking about it during the farewell had been.

But she did hate that she hadn't got to touch him one last time. That she hadn't gotten to feel his lips against hers one last time as they shared a goodbye kiss. That there'd been no additional time for talking, for asking him about what had happened to him.

But then she'd think of Joss and the panicky, got-to-escape, how-could-I-not-have-told-him? feelings would take over again and she'd heavy-foot the gas pedal. She'd gotten home in record time.

"There you go again," Savannah accused, eyeing her from across the living room where she held her baby, nursing her. "Something happened this weekend."

Chrissie looked at her friend with an obviously guilty expression because her friend's eyes widened.

"Something did happen!" Savannah exclaimed, louder than she should have as Amelia stopped nursing and whimpered. Savannah quickly settled her daughter and whispered, "Tell me."

Chrissie looked down at the sleeping little boy curled in her arms. Joss had been so excited when she'd gotten there, had given her a welcome home card he and his "Auntie" Savannah had made. Savannah had insisted they stay for dinner, during which her husband Charlie had been called into the hospital and had to leave. When they'd finished eating, while Savannah had recounted Joss's adventures over the weekend, Joss had climbed into Chrissie's lap and dozed off almost immediately. She hadn't minded. She loved these moments of holding him close, of snuggling his little body, and feeling his heart next to hers.

Something she'd denied Trace from ever knowing by not telling him about his son. Guilt stung her eyes and she sniffled.

She was not going to cry. She wasn't. No way.

"Tell me," Savannah insisted a little louder when Chrissie still hesitated.

"I…" What did she say to Savannah? How did she begin to explain to her best friend that she'd had a repeat of the weekend that had given her Joss?

Well, hopefully, not a full repeat as they'd used protection every time, and surely odds wouldn't be on her getting pregnant twice while protected?

Her head spun for a brief moment. The thought of being pregnant with Trace's baby again didn't repel the way it should have. Maybe it was because Joss was curled in her arms and she'd missed him so much. Maybe it was because Savannah was nursing Amelia and had never looked happier than she did these days.

Maybe it was something more.

"He was there," she confessed.

"He?" Eyes wide, Savannah dropped her gaze to Joss. "The guy from before?"

Face on fire, Chrissie nodded.

"You had sex with him again!"

"Shh!" Chrissie winced and fought the urge to cover Joss's ears. As irrational as it was, she didn't want her son to hear this conversation. Not that he was aware of anything going on around him. He was out for the count.

"You slept with Joss's dad?" Savannah stage-whispered.

Knowing she'd eventually tell Savannah everything, Chrissie nodded. She really needed to talk, to let out some of the strong emotions flowing through her. Maybe Savannah could make sense of them. Chrissie sure couldn't.

"I did and it was great. Better than I remembered."

Savannah smiled. "That's wonderful."

Chrissie could see the matchmaking wheels spinning in her best friend's head.

"It was wonderful, but *was* is the key word. It was just a fling. Just like before."

Savannah frowned. "What do you mean?"

"We agreed to have a no-strings-attached affair for the weekend and that's what we had. End of story."

"No, not end of story, because you have strings."

"No, I don't," Chrissie denied. Yeah, she had feelings for Trace. How could she not, but those weren't strings. They were...tiny threads of nothingness.

"Hello, you are holding the biggest string there is."

She shook her head. "Joss isn't a string between Trace and me."

"Trace? That's his name?"

Chrissie nodded. Hearing her best friend say Trace's name for the first time felt good in an odd sort of way. As if it somehow made him more real. As if she hadn't imagined this past weekend and the man who had rocked her world.

Of course she hadn't. Proof really did lie in her arms.

"He doesn't know about Joss." Why she blurted that particular tidbit out Chrissie wasn't sure. But she did blurt it out. She also had fire burning her face.

Savannah's thin brows veed. "Why didn't you tell him?"

Wishing she could fan her face, she shrugged. "Probably for the same reasons you didn't tell Charlie you were pregnant those first few months."

Chrissie's comment had Savannah relenting a little, but only a little.

"Chrissie, you need to tell him. He is Joss's father. I know I didn't tell Charlie to begin with, but

I should have. The longer I waited, the more difficult admitting the truth became."

Savannah had found out she was pregnant on
the very day Charlie had told her he had taken
a job two hours away and was moving. Without
her. It had taken a while for Savannah and Charlie
to work out their differences, but now Chrissie's
friend had her happily-ever-after.

Chrissie winced. "We were only supposed to
be an affair. He doesn't want to be burdened with
a kid."

Her friend fixed her with a glare. "Is that how
you feel about Joss?"

"Of course not!" She tightened her hold around
her sleeping son. "Joss is my whole world."

Savannah gave her another sharp look as if to
say, *Exactly.*

"Fine, I see your point, but you don't understand. He works with Doctors Around the World
and he's leaving soon."

"Then you really should have told him while
you were in Atlanta."

In between their sneaky kisses or perhaps by the
stream? Or maybe right before she'd left Atlanta.

*See you later, Trace. And, oh, by the way, we
have a three-year-old son you know nothing about.*

Wrong. She shouldn't have told him anything.
He was leaving. He didn't want kids. She'd done
him a favor.

"Does this have to do with your father and what happened when you were young?"

"No," she denied. "Maybe." She realized the tears she wasn't going to shed had made their way down her cheeks. "Possibly. I don't know, Savannah. I wanted to tell him, but he told me four years ago that he planned never to marry or have children. He still feels that way. Still, I thought about telling him of Joss but never could say the words. He wouldn't really take Joss away from me. At least, I don't believe he would. But my mom never would have left me with my dad if she'd thought he would kidnap me either."

Not that Chrissie had realized at first what her dad had done. He'd told her they were going on a special vacation together and she'd always craved her father's attention, so she'd been a happy little girl. It was only days later, when he still hadn't let her call her mother, would get angry that she wanted to, had slapped her when she'd started crying for her mother, that she'd started questioning their vacation that wasn't much more than sleeping in different cars, cars she'd later learned he'd stolen along their way, and long hours on the road.

"Most men aren't like your father, Chrissie." Savannah shuddered and kissed the top of Amelia's head. "Thank God."

"Trace lives a very different life from most men, Savannah. He's with DAW and goes into dangerous places. He is a good man, would feel obligated. Not knowing is better for him."

Only, if the roles were reversed, she'd want to know. She'd want to be a part of Joss's life. Would Trace?

"I don't have his number or any way of getting in touch with him," she said as much for her benefit as for Savannah's.

She didn't have Trace's number. There had been no need for number exchanges at the event. Not before and not this time. To have exchanged numbers would have implied a future they didn't share.

Only, she did have Alexis's cell-phone number and she knew the beautiful Atlanta cardiologist had Trace's number.

"Chrissie, I can see how much you are struggling with this. Which tells me what I need to know. You have to tell him."

Feeling overwhelmed with emotion and fatigue, she shook her head. Too much had happened in Atlanta. She needed to think, to figure out exactly what she wanted to say to Trace, to be sure of whatever decisions she made because those decisions forever impacted her son.

And Trace.

CHAPTER NINE

CHRISSIE DIDN'T KNOW what she wanted.

She didn't want the traditional happily-ever-after. She didn't fool herself that she'd ever have that and, honestly, she wasn't in a rush to search for it. She was content to raise Joss and after he left to forge his own life, then she'd worry about her personal life, or lack thereof.

Overall, she was pretty happy with her life as it was.

At least, she had been.

Before her weekend in Atlanta with Trace.

Now, there was a restlessness that moved through her.

A week had gone by.

He'd probably already left Atlanta for some deprived part of the world where he was selflessly helping others.

She couldn't berate him for that.

What he was doing was admirable, heroic even.

He didn't know he was missing the precious youth of his son.

Because he didn't know he had a son.

Because she hadn't told him. What kind of horribly selfish person was she?

One who had been kidnapped by her father, an inner voice defended.

Somehow the defense kept falling flat and never resolving Chrissie's growing guilt.

"Why are you crying, Mommy?"

Chrissie blinked at Joss. She'd spread a blanket in their backyard to read a nursing magazine while he played in his sandbox with a shovel, pail, and myriad toy cars and trucks. Apparently, he'd noticed his mother's tears.

Which was more than she could say for herself.

She hadn't realized she was crying. Again. She'd cried way too often over the past week.

Over guilt, she told herself, not because she was missing Trace, not because of the ache in her chest at the thought of never seeing him again.

"Are you sad?" he asked, wiping his gritty fingers across her cheek to clear her tears.

"A little," she answered him, bending to press a kiss to the top of his blond head. "Mommy was thinking about a friend."

Who wasn't really a friend at all, but a lover.

An amazing lover whom she missed.

She missed Trace. Which made no sense. She'd known she wouldn't see him beyond the event weekend. But she missed him.

Not because of his out-of-this-world bedroom skills, but because of his quick smile and wit, the way his eyes lit up when they met hers, the intelligent conversations they'd shared.

Okay, so she missed his bedroom skills, too.

"We could go see your friend," Joss offered with

his three-year-old's logic. "Then you wouldn't be sad no more."

She smiled at him. "*Any* more, and you're right."

If only she believed that, but seeing Trace again, if that was even a possibility, might destroy everything she knew and loved. Was she willing to risk it?

Was it fair to Joss, to Trace, if she wasn't?

Wasn't that the real cloud hanging over her the past week? The knowledge that whatever she decided would have such a terrible impact on the person she loved most in the world, on herself, on Trace?

Chrissie loved her job in the CVICU most days. She'd operated as the charge nurse on the unit for a couple of years and really liked the team of nurses and doctors she worked with. They were a good crew.

Especially now that her bestie was back working on an as-needed basis. Like today.

"I'm so glad you're here," she told Savannah. "I know you miss Amelia, but you made my life better by coming in."

Savannah grinned. "The timing was perfect as Charlie was off work today so he could be at home with Amelia. It'll give them some good bonding time together. I'll just have to sneak away a couple of times to pump milk, but other than that I'm happy to be back in the land of adulthood."

Staying home with Joss hadn't been an option. Chrissie had worked like crazy during her pregnancy, saving and putting back as much as she could to cover the expenses of a baby. Fortunately, she'd always been frugal and had bought her little house not long after she'd graduated from nursing school. It was down the road from her mother and, although nothing fancy, she loved her two-bed, one-bath home in its quiet little neighborhood. All of which had made welcoming Joss into her life much easier. Her mother adored her grandson. Her mother had helped her tremendously as she'd made the transition from single woman to single mom, offering to babysit and a shoulder to cry on.

She'd not needed the shoulder, but had welcomed her mother's help with Joss while she'd been at work because she'd hated leaving him. Knowing he was with her mother had at least lightened that guilt. Maybe it was a guilt all working moms felt—the need to be at work and to do a good job there and the need to be with their child and to be a good mom.

Regardless, she was grateful for her mother, and pleased that Savannah had been able to spend the first months of her daughter's life with Amelia.

"We're pretty booked up. I've got a room and you're assigned to two," she told her friend, then let the nurse who'd stayed over to cover until Savannah could get there give her report.

In the meanwhile, Chrissie went to check her

patient. A young man in his twenties who'd had a valve replacement the day before.

The boy was still on the ventilator and asleep when Chrissie went in to check him. His father sat in a chair next to the bed and opened his eyes when she entered the room.

"Hi," she greeted the tired-looking man.

The man nodded acknowledgment, but turned his attention immediately to the pale young man lying in the bed with multiple tubes and wires attached to his body. "How is he?"

Chrissie scanned over the telemetry. "Still holding his own." She smiled at the man empathetically. "He should start stirring some soon."

"I hope so. I miss seeing this kid's smile. He's my whole world."

"I understand. I have a three-year-old son. He's my whole world, too."

The man continued, obviously needing to talk. "He has to be okay."

"Dr. Flowers expects him to recover fully," she reminded him.

"I pray so." The man raked his fingers through his salt-and-pepper hair. "We've only connected a few years ago. Now, I can't imagine my life without him."

"Oh?" Chrissie gazed at the man, who was leaning forward, staring at the rise and fall of the young man's bandaged chest.

He sighed, his gaze flickering to hers for a brief

moment. "His mother and I weren't married. She got ill a few years back and told him about me. After she passed, he looked me up." Wincing, he shook off a memory. "I was a jerk to begin with. I didn't believe he was mine."

At Chrissie's grimace, the man elaborated.

"How could I have known? His mother and I only dated for a short while and then I never saw her again. I never even thought about her until he showed up in my life almost twenty years later. If only she'd told me."

Chrissie's chest tightened to where she could barely breathe. "What would you have done?"

Startled at her question, the man met her gaze. "I'm not sure, but I do know my son would have known who I was, not just my name, and that in some shape, form, or fashion, I'd have been a father to him. She should have told me. For her not to have, and to have deprived me of knowing my kid, was selfish." Red heightened his cheeks, contrasting with his otherwise pale face. "It's probably wrong to be angry at the dead, but I struggle with it every day."

With her insides shaking, Chrissie finished checking her patient.

When she left the room, she was sweating.

Yet icy cold inside.

If only she'd told me. For her not to have...was selfish.

Was that a sentiment Trace would someday feel? That she'd been selfish to deprive him of Joss?

It was how she'd feel if she were the one missing their son's life.

She glanced around the CVICU. For a morning that had started a bit chaotic due to being short-handed, now everything was, for the moment, calm and smooth, thanks to Savannah coming in and covering their short-staffed situation.

With clammy hands, she pulled out her phone, then went into an empty patient room and pulled the sliding glass door closed.

She had to call Alexis, then Trace. Now. She couldn't wait another minute, couldn't second-guess herself or let the past, or her baggage, interfere with doing what she knew she had to do.

Trace had gotten his next assignment with DAW. He'd start out in Africa again for at least six months. Unfortunately, he wouldn't be leaving for almost three weeks and that had him restless. He was ready to get back to work.

He'd met Bud and Agnes for lunch at a downtown Atlanta restaurant to spend some time with them prior to leaving. A week had passed since the fund-raiser event and he'd not seen them since. Bud always took Agnes on a mini-vacation the week after the event and they'd just gotten home the day before.

He enjoyed listening to the details of their

cruise. Years ago, he'd met them on a regular basis for lunch and realized as he sat across from them how much he missed doing so.

"Have you talked to Chrissie?"

Agnes's question caught him off guard.

"We made no plans to stay in touch. You know that."

The older woman looked at her husband and shook her head. "Young people these days are so blind to what's right in front of them."

Bud smiled indulgently at his wife. "What's that, honey?"

"Don't tell me you didn't see what I saw at the event, because I know better."

Bud patted her hand. "Agnes, if the boy says he doesn't want to stay in touch with the girl then he doesn't want to stay in touch with her."

"No, that's not what that means, Bud. It means he's not smart enough to go after her."

"Agnes, I leave in a couple of weeks," he reminded her. "Even if I wanted to go after Chrissie, what would be the point?"

An *aha!* look brightened her face. "Do you want to?"

Good ol' Agnes. She didn't beat around the bush.

"No, Agnes, I don't want to pursue a woman." Which might not be a hundred percent the truth because he had thought about Chrissie a lot over the past week.

But he always came back to the same conclusion. She'd left without saying goodbye for a reason. Because she'd known, like him, that they had no future together.

He couldn't justify interfering in her life when he'd be on another continent. What were they supposed to do? Teleconference stay in touch? He wouldn't do that to her.

"See, I told you there was more between them than met the eye," Agnes spoke up, nudging her husband, and sending Trace an I-told-you-so look.

"Oh, there was plenty that met the eye," Bud countered. "But whatever was between them was exactly like the boy said, between him and the girl."

Agnes just shook her head at her husband.

His cell phone rang and Trace was grateful for the escape from the current conversation.

"Sorry." He pulled out the phone and answered.

"Trace?" a familiar female voice asked. "This is Chrissie."

His heart pounded, but a repeated "Hello," was all he said due to the curious stares he was receiving from the couple across the restaurant table.

"Is this a bad time?" she asked, her voice almost sounding as if she hoped he said it was.

"Could've been worse."

"Oh." She paused a moment. "I...maybe I could call back at a more convenient time."

"There's no need," he assured, mouthing "sorry" to Bud and Agnes. "What can I do for you?"

"I…I want to see you."

His heart leapt, but he kept his expression neutral under Agnes's eagle eyes. Not that she knew who he was talking to, but somehow she'd always had a way of figuring things out.

"What's changed?" he asked. After all, she'd left without saying goodbye to him.

"I'd rather not say over the phone."

"You're in Atlanta?" He was going for nonchalant, partly because of Agnes's hawk eyes and partly because he didn't want to sound overly eager to Chrissie.

Regardless of his efforts, Agnes was looking more and more interested in his conversation. He'd really rather not have to explain his phone call and have her asking questions he probably wouldn't be able to answer.

"No, I'm in Chattanooga, but…"

"You expect me to drive there?"

"Would you?" She sounded hopeful. "That would definitely be easier given the circumstances."

What circumstances? Part of Trace wanted to agree, but the curious stares of the couple across the table from him had him holding his guns.

"I'm a busy man." He was coming off as a jerk. Then again, he hadn't been the one to drive away without so much as a *see ya*. A little anger and bitterness was to be expected, surely?

"I know," she admitted, sounding remorseful and making him feel every bit the prize jerk he was being.

"I wasn't sure if you were still in the States," she continued. "Are you?"

"I'm in Atlanta still."

"Oh. That's good."

"Why are you calling?" he asked, because she was definitely stalling by talking in circles.

"I had a baby."

No longer caring that Agnes and Bud were listening in on every word he said, Trace frowned at her blurted-out shocker.

"That's impossible. It's only been a week."

If he'd thought about his response, he'd have known that was not what she meant but her comment had caught him so off guard he hadn't been thinking. Maybe he hadn't been breathing either because he felt light-headed.

"Not now," she clarified, her voice shaky. "I... I had a baby before coming to Atlanta this time, Trace."

Chrissie had a baby. She'd been curvier than before, but he'd just figured she'd put on a few pounds. Definitely, he'd never suspected she'd given birth. He didn't recall any noticeable stretch marks on her belly, but then, not all women got many stretch marks. Plus, he'd been so paranoid about his own scars that he might not have noticed.

Or so caught up in his physical need that he might not have noticed because he'd wanted her something fierce. They'd taken things slower in his tent, but they'd been in the dark and had needed to feel their way.

Chrissie had a baby.

Chrissie was a mother.

His brain reeled at the implications.

"That's why you just left? Because you have a baby?"

Agnes's eyes were saucers now and Bud was likely going to have bruises from how she was elbowing him.

"Yes." Chrissie sounded flustered.

"I don't understand why that meant you couldn't say goodbye to me."

"You and I have a baby, Trace." She enunciated each word with great clarity. "A three-year-old son."

She kept talking, but her language might as well have been foreign because Trace couldn't make out her words, just bits and pieces of sounds that echoed through his mind.

You and I have a baby. A three-year-old son.

He was her baby's father?

He was a father?

She was lying.

They didn't have a son.
He didn't have a child.
Only it *was* possible...

CHAPTER TEN

CHRISSIE HAD WORKED five twelve-hour shifts straight and was exhausted when she picked Joss up from her mother's that evening. Still, she put on a happy face for him, fed him, then gave him his bath.

Three bedtime stories and lots of giggles later she put him to bed, then went to shower.

When her phone rang, she figured it was Savannah to check on her after her mini-meltdown at work that day. Calling Trace and blurting out the truth wasn't exactly what she'd planned, at least, not over the phone. She could hardly believe that she'd let a patient get to her that intensely. She'd call Savannah back when she got out of the shower.

Letting the hot water sluice over her body and wash away the day's grime, she wished she could as easily wash away the stress. If only it were that easy.

A downpour wouldn't wash away her day's stresses. Not today. Stress she'd caused herself by calling Trace. Why had she called him?

Because a pitiful man sitting over his unconscious son's body had gotten to her as she'd listened to his story. Bits and pieces of that story had resonated a little too close. Had reinforced what had been eating at her from the moment she'd laid eyes on Trace again.

She had to tell him about Joss. Not to was wrong. She hadn't needed to hear the man's words to know that. But maybe she'd needed to hear them to make her get beyond the past and act.

Because she was scared. And selfish.

When she got out of the shower, the number showing on the cell phone wasn't Savannah's.

It was the number she'd programmed into her phone after Alexis had given it to her. The number she had called earlier that day because she'd gotten so emotionally tangled up that the need to call him had about done her in.

Trace's number.

He'd called.

Her phone vibrated in her hand and played a series of musical notes.

Correction. He was calling. Trace was calling.

With shaky fingers, she slid her fingertip across the phone screen to answer the call. "Hello."

"Chrissie."

"Trace." Their one word responses couldn't go on, so she added, "Good to hear from you."

"Is it?"

She winced. Not quite sure how to take his comment, she opted to ignore it. It was good to hear from him compared to not hearing from him, but she didn't really know what to say.

"Why are you calling, Trace?"

"You thought I wouldn't after the bombshell you dropped?"

Heat crawled up Chrissie's neck.

"You got off the phone with me rather abruptly. I wasn't sure what to expect." Ha. He'd essentially hung up on her, leaving her a bumbling mess that Savannah had found crying in the empty patient room she'd called him from.

Ugh. How she hated the tangled mess she found herself in. Stupid conscience. Stupid her for going to Atlanta. Stupid. Stupid. Stupid.

Everything had been just fine until she'd seen Trace again. She'd been happy, content with her life with Joss. Then she'd had to go and mess everything up by going back to the place where it all started.

The moment she'd seen Trace she should have left.

Only part of her acknowledged she'd gone to Atlanta with the hopes of possibly seeing him again.

Which meant what exactly?

She'd brought this mess tumbling down upon herself for sure.

"I needed to process what you said."

That she could understand. She hadn't meant to tell him over the phone. She'd meant to set up a time they could meet, talk, that she could tell him about Joss, show him a picture, let him decide how he wanted to proceed with becoming a part of Joss's life.

If he wanted to be a part of Joss's life.

"Have you?" she whispered, her voice twisting up in her throat.

His sigh was palpable across the phone. "As much as I can."

Chrissie shifted the phone to her opposite hand and pulled a baggy T-shirt over her wet head, thinking that might help her feel less uncomfortable talking to him. Getting dressed sure couldn't hurt, because standing wrapped only in a towel was doing nothing for her nerves.

His silence wasn't, either.

"And?" she finally asked, pulling on a pair of panties, and carrying her towel back to the bathroom and hanging it over the side of the tub.

She wasn't sure she wanted to know what Trace had concluded, but was ready to prepare for whatever the near future was about to bring, because obviously she'd reached a point where she was no longer able to deal with her guilty conscience.

"I want to meet him."

She wasn't sure if the noise that escaped her was a sigh in relief or a whimper of despair. Maybe a deformed bit of both.

She went into her living room, sat on her sofa, and hugged her knees up to her. "When?"

"Now."

"Now?"

"You heard me."

"I… He's asleep." Not that that made any sense, but it was what she said. Her head was being bombarded with so many thoughts that nothing made sense. Maybe it never would again.

"Maybe asleep is better."

"You're in Atlanta."

"I'm not."

He wasn't in Atlanta. Her breath came in rapid little breaths she had to consciously stop by inhaling a deep, slow one.

"You're here." It wasn't a question. Trace was there. In Tennessee. In Chattanooga.

"Parked at a gas station. I want to come to your house."

Trace was here! She gripped her phone tighter.

"I just got out of the shower. I'm not even dressed." Panties and an oversized T-shirt didn't count. Not where Trace was concerned. "I wasn't expecting company."

"I'm not coming to see you, Chrissie," he reminded her. "I want to see the boy."

The boy? Probably because of her already raw nerves, but his calling Joss "the boy" irritated.

"His name is Joss," she reminded him with enough force to make her point. "I told you that."

"Joss," he said. "I want to see Joss."

"I…" She took a deep breath. "Okay, fine. Give me fifteen minutes and I'll let you in. Be quiet, though, because he really is asleep."

She gave him the address, then hung up and pulled on a pair of sweats, put her bra back on beneath her shirt so she didn't feel so exposed, and was combing through her damp hair when she heard his car in her driveway.

Five minutes. Ugh. Of course he'd come straight there, even though she'd asked for fifteen minutes. Maybe he'd sit and wait the extra ten minutes she'd asked for—minutes in which she'd planned to do a quick run-through clean of her house.

No such luck.

Within seconds, he was knocking on her front door.

Her heart skipped a couple of beats and her head spun.

Trace was at her house. Knew about Joss. Was about to see their son for the first time.

A wave of intense protectiveness swept over her, making her question every move she'd made that had led up to this moment. Making her wonder if she should snatch up her son and run.

Good grief. Where had that thought come from? She was not like her father. She'd never do that.

Only, hadn't she already kept their son away from Trace?

Remorse and guilt flooded her as she opened her front door and saw the pale, almost ill-looking man standing on her porch.

What had she done?

* * *

Sorrow lit in Chrissie's eyes, but at the moment Trace didn't care.

She'd called him with some trumped-up story about having had his son.

How was that even possible?

He knew how, but that he could have fathered a son and not known for years just seemed unfathomable. That she would have kept that from him was unfathomable.

He still wasn't sure he believed her.

And if the truth was that he had fathered her son?

Well, she'd be a wealthy lady because his parents would be thrilled to hand her over whatever she wanted in exchange for her precious offspring.

Not that he'd let them.

Not that he thought Chrissie the gold-digger type anyway.

Then again, maybe he'd been overseas too long.

His head hurt. His neck and shoulder muscles ached with the tension that had struck him from the moment she'd uttered her life-shattering revelation.

He didn't know what he'd do if she'd told the truth. What he'd say. At the moment, he just wanted to get past the woman in the doorway and to the child she was claiming was his.

He'd look at the boy and know, wouldn't he?

Surely a father would look at his child and inherently know "that's mine."

"I asked for fifteen minutes," Chrissie said, crossing her arms across her chest. She'd been telling the truth about just getting out of the shower. Her hair was damp, her skin still had that just-washed glow, and the scent of her shampoo permeated his senses despite his state of mind.

Yeah, she'd asked for fifteen minutes, but he'd not been able to wait. Funny, but for four years he hadn't known the kid existed, and now that he did he hadn't been able to delay another ten minutes.

She shouldn't have asked him to. Not after having already made him wait so long to see what she claimed belonged to him.

"Where is he?"

"Asleep. I told you—"

"I want to see him." He was being blunt, was being rude, even, with his brusqueness, but if Chrissie had given birth to his son and not told him, then he hated to consider the ramifications.

She didn't move out of the doorway, just stared at him with a mixture of fear, uncertainty, and protectiveness.

"What are you planning to do?"

Good question and not one he knew the answer to. Just that he needed to see the child and he hadn't been able to wait.

"I won't let you hurt him, Trace."

Trace clenched his fingers into his palms. "Seriously? You think I drove all this way to hurt a kid? Just what kind of opinion do you have of me, Chrissie?"

Remorse softened her expression a little.

"The kind that meant you kept my son from me for four years?"

His voice rose in pitch and she shushed him, making his insides bristle further.

"Please don't wake him. He doesn't know about you. He wouldn't understand if he woke and you were here."

"He normally sleeps through when you have male company?" Yeah, he was being a sarcastic jerk, but he wasn't in a forgiving mood.

"Not that it's any of your business, but I don't have male company."

"Right."

She held her stance. "The only guy in my life is Joss and he's three years old and asleep in his bed. There's not been anyone else, not since you."

His gaze narrowed. "Since four years ago?"

"If you mean, have I gone on dates, then yes, Trace, I have gone on a few. If you mean, have I had sex with anyone besides you in the past four years, then the answer is no, I haven't."

He found that difficult to believe. She was a sensual woman, so responsive and passionate. But he didn't want to think about that, or whether or not she'd been with anyone other than him. At the moment, his priorities lay elsewhere.

"Your sleeping habits over the past four years really aren't my business." Yet the thought that she'd not been with anyone since him did please him, as crazy as that was. Then again, at the moment, everything, every thought, felt crazy. "Where is his room?"

Chrissie's lower lip disappeared between her teeth at his question. She stepped aside, allowing him to enter the house.

"I'll show you."

Taking note of the photos on the walls of a healthy, blond-haired little boy who had no issues smiling for a camera, Trace followed Chrissie to the short hallway and into a room lit only by a superhero nightlight.

A curled-up little body lay in a plastic car bed with a mattress in the center. The bed sat low to the floor and Trace knelt beside it, focusing through the low light on the tow-headed child.

The sleeping boy faced where Trace knelt and he could make out his features. Trace sensed Chrissie beside him, could sense her nervousness, but didn't look her way. What did she think he was going to do? Grab the kid and run?

Long lashes fanned across the boy's cheeks and he had a full lower lip that made him think of Chrissie's pouty mouth.

Was the boy his?

Trace's blood felt like acid as it moved through

him. Shouldn't he know? Shouldn't he be able to immediately tell?

He reached out to touch him and Chrissie moved to stop him. He cut his gaze toward her and his look must have said everything, because she backed away without a word.

Trace touched Joss.

His son?

Hadn't he known when he'd seen the eyes staring back at him from the photos on Chrissie's walls?

Hard emotions slammed into him.

He was touching his son.

Joss was his.

He gently cupped the boy's head in his palm in a caress and trembled at the enormity of the moment.

This was his son. He was touching a living, breathing human child he'd helped make.

Next to him, Chrissie made a noise and he realized she was crying. Louder than she should be if they were not to wake the boy. He gave her a look that said to stop, but that only made things worse as she broke into a full-out sob.

The little boy shifted in his sleep, moving against Trace's hand.

With one last stroke of his fingertips across the soft blond hair, Trace stood, grabbed Chrissie's wrist, and pulled her from the room.

"Were you trying to wake him?" he accused when they got back to the living room.

She shook her head.

"If he'd awakened and I was there with you crying it would have traumatized him. Is that what you were hoping for? To make him not trust me from the beginning?"

"No," she denied, looking horrified at his accusation. "Of course not. How could you think that?"

"How could I think otherwise? I have a son who doesn't know me from a stranger because you kept him from me."

She winced at his accusation. "I didn't know where you were."

"Did you look?"

Guilt written all over her face, she closed her eyes. "No."

"Then don't tell me you didn't know where I was. I wouldn't have been that difficult to track down. You knew I lived in Atlanta...that I'd been at the CCPO event. All you had to do was ask Agnes and she'd have gotten word to me."

"I can't change the past, Trace. I thought you wouldn't want to know."

"Why would you think that?"

"You're the one who told me you didn't want a relationship, didn't want children, *ever*. I was a weekend fling. Someone you'd had a good time with and nothing more. We weren't dating, or an item, or involved in any way. I wasn't supposed to get pregnant."

She was right.

"Did you get pregnant on purpose?"

Her chin jutted forward. "You know I didn't."

"Why did you suddenly decide to tell me?"

"It wasn't suddenly." She wiped at the tears still running down her cheeks. "I'd been thinking about it since first seeing you in the medical tent again."

Right. That was why she'd not bothered to tell him while they'd been in Atlanta.

"I'm staying here," he announced, surprising both him and her with his decision.

Her eyes were wide. "Here as in my house?"

He nodded.

"I don't think—"

"That's right. You don't think. Nor do you get to have a say in this. You have kept my son from me for four years."

She collapsed onto the sofa as if her legs would no longer hold her. Her head drooped low, the tears starting again full force.

"I am going to get to know my son the best I can in what time I have left before I leave and you're going to help me do it so it causes him as little stress as possible."

"How am I supposed to do that?" she asked, looking up at him through her red-rimmed eyes.

"By making me a welcomed houseguest, by being friendly to me so he doesn't pick up on any negative feelings, by telling him the truth."

"You want me to tell him that you're his father?" She sounded horrified.

"You think it better to lie to him and tell him I'm some random guy you've decided to let move in?"

"There's not room in my house for you, Trace."

He glanced around the living room. "This is a mansion compared to some of the hellholes where I've worked over the past four years. I'll be fine."

Not that he thought for one second she was concerned about his comfort. She didn't want him there. Too bad. He wanted every second possible with his son, to get to know the boy and for his son to get to know him. He'd figure the rest out later. For now that was the only game plan he had.

"But—"

"I'm staying and we're not lying about who I am."

"But—" she repeated.

"You'll tell him tomorrow when he wakes up that I am his father."

"But—"

"I don't have time for games, Chrissie. I'll be leaving for Africa soon. In a couple of weeks."

"Oh."

"Yeah, oh. He'll stay with me while you go to work." Which just occurred to him. "Do you work tomorrow?"

Staying with the boy on day one would be awkward, but he'd figure it out.

"No, I'm off for the next four days."

"That's good. That will give him time to get used to me before he stays with me." And then

Trace would have to leave soon thereafter. How long would it be before he'd be back in the States? Six months? A year? Maybe longer?

"He's not staying alone with you."

"He is." Trace cut his gaze to Chrissie's watery-eyed one. Under other circumstances he could feel badly for her, would have wanted to comfort her.

These weren't other circumstances.

CHAPTER ELEVEN

SEEING TRACE'S PAIN and frustration hurt.

She couldn't argue with him. Not when in many ways he was right.

She had kept their son away from him, something that no matter how she tried to make up for, she'd never be able to. In some ways she was no better than her father.

She could remind him that he'd said he didn't want children, but she'd never presented him with the option of wanting Joss.

"Fine. Stay here." She gestured to the sofa. "I'll grab a pillow and a blanket."

He shook his head. "I don't need them. You do."

Was he kidding? Her brow lifted. "I'm sleeping on the sofa?"

He nodded. "If Joss wakes up in the middle of the night, it might scare him to find a strange man on the sofa. Which means I can't stay on the sofa. Unless you've got another bedroom where you can put me, I'm taking your room where I can lock the door to prevent him from finding me unexpectedly."

He was putting her on the sofa and taking her bed.

"I haven't changed my sheets this week."

He didn't look impressed. "I've survived worse than dirty sheets."

She'd done this. She'd set this wheel into motion. No, she hadn't really expected him to show up at her house and announce he was staying, but it wasn't as if she'd expected to tell him they'd had a child and him to say, *That's nice* and never to hear from him again.

Or maybe she had.

Maybe she'd simply been appeasing her conscience and had hoped he'd stay away so she could go on with the way things had been before seeing him again.

"What am I supposed to tell my mother?"

For the briefest of moments, she thought she'd reached him. But after that flash of indecision, his expression steeled again.

"The truth."

The truth?

Her mother had never pushed too hard for her to spill the details of how she'd ended up pregnant. She'd always been a good daughter, had rarely bucked her mother's wishes. She had probably guessed that her daughter had gotten pregnant while at the CCPO event four years ago. When she'd burst into tears when asked about Joss's father, her mother had accepted her answer that he was no longer in the picture and getting help from him wasn't an option. She'd never asked since.

How would she react to him now living in her house?

To his just showing up out of the blue?

Well, maybe, not so out of the blue. Her family knew she'd been in Atlanta for CCPO again a week ago.

Heaviness tugged at her shoulders.

"How long do you plan to stay?"

He shrugged. "Until I have to leave."

How would that affect Joss? For Trace to come waltzing in, play the role of daddy for a few weeks, then disappear again?

"You can't just come into Joss's life, then walk away as if he doesn't exist. He wouldn't understand that."

He crossed his arms and stared at her as if she were a pesky fly. "Not once have I said anything about walking away from my son as if he doesn't exist."

She crossed her arms, too, and did her best to stare him down the way he was her. And not to react to his *my son* because those words scared her a little. He hadn't said "our son."

She swallowed the lump forming in her throat. "You plan to stay in Chattanooga?"

Because she wouldn't acknowledge that he might mean something other than his staying here.

She wouldn't let him take Joss to Africa. She wasn't sure she could stop him forever, but for the moment she was Joss's legal guardian and had final say.

"You know that isn't the case. I'm booked on a flight a couple of weeks from now. In the meantime, I'm going to get to know my son. He's going to get to know me and you are going to facilitate that so it goes as smoothly as possible given the unfortunate circumstances."

His tone brooked no argument, nor did his retreating back as he stepped outside.

Heart racing, she ran to the front door, watched him walk around to the front seat of an expensive-looking SUV. He grabbed an overnight bag from the front floorboard, then headed back her way.

"Miss me?" he quipped, looking way more relaxed and comfortable than he should considering he was invading her home as an unwanted houseguest and as a man who had just met his son for the first time a few minutes ago.

"You wish," she countered, glaring at him.

Not acknowledging her quip, he stepped around her, headed toward the hallway, then paused. "You need anything out of here before I crash?"

He was really going to sleep in her room, in her bed, and let her take the sofa? Sure, his reasons made sense, but still...

"Yes." She pushed past him and went into her room, grabbed one of the pillows off her full-sized bed, then glanced around the room. The room was about twelve by twelve and dominated by the queen-sized bed. There was a stack of books on her night stand, a mix of hers and Joss's. Some clean clothes were draped over a wicker chair that had been her grandmother's, waiting on her to hang them in her closet. At least she'd semi-made her bed that morning.

Then again, what did it matter? She hadn't invited him. He wasn't her guest. If her house was a total wreck, tough.

On that note, she turned, expecting to see him standing behind her, but he wasn't. He'd stopped by Joss's room, probably to stare at their son.

She took a deep breath, pulled a blanket out of a plastic bin from under her bed.

This time when she turned to leave her room, seeing Trace standing in her bedroom doorway caused her heart to stop.

Or pretty darn close.

Who would have thought Trace would be in her house, standing in her bedroom doorway?

Never in her wildest dreams had she thought that would ever happen.

Because for all her fear over his meeting Joss, for all her nervousness at what the future held, the man was breathtaking.

Which didn't sit well because she needed all her wits about her, not to get distracted by his soulful eyes, broad shoulders, and overflowing charisma. Not that he'd shown much charm since arriving at her house.

Determined to protect her heart, she narrowed her gaze at him. "The bathroom is down the hallway. Stay out of my drawers."

He laughed and it was a dry, harsh sound. "No worries, Chrissie."

She wasn't sure they were talking about the same drawers, but what did it matter? He'd made his point loud and clear.

He was there because of their son. Not her.

Trace had slept very little and was wide awake as the first streams of morning light came through Chrissie's unshaded windows.

Part of him felt like a jerk for taking her room. Another truly believed he should be behind locked doors in case Joss woke prior to him and Chrissie. He didn't want to scare the kid.

The kid.

His kid.

He hadn't really questioned Chrissie. Logic said he should get a paternity test. Not to would just be foolish on his part. But when he'd knelt beside the bed staring at the peacefully sleeping boy in the dimly lit room, he'd not been thinking, *What if?* He'd been thinking, *That's mine.*

Because he wanted the boy to be his.

He'd not planned to have children, so how much he wanted Joss to be his didn't make logical sense.

How could he so desperately want what Chrissie had told him to be true?

He believed her.

All night he'd battled between anger, a sense of betrayal, uncertainty, and awe that he'd fathered a child.

Restless, he pushed the sheet back and got up.

Going to the living room, panic hit him when he saw the empty sofa. Had she taken off in the middle of the night?

Turning, he went to Joss's room, pushed open the door and stopped short at what he saw.

Chrissie's small frame was curled on the car bed with her son's little body pressed up against hers. The little boy's hand rested on his mother's.

Morning light lit the room, and with him lying next to Chrissie it was easy to see his resemblance to his mother.

Same blond hair, same beautiful porcelain skin.

He sat down in a rocking chair, careful to keep the chair from squeaking, and watched the sleeping mother and child.

His child.

His and Chrissie's child.

As angry as he was at her for not telling him about Joss, he couldn't imagine anyone that he'd rather have as a mother of his child. Certainly, Chrissie had haunted him while he'd been overseas.

While she'd been raising their child.

While he'd been lying in a hospital recovering,

she'd been here, with their son. And he hadn't known.

Another surge of betrayal burst through him that she hadn't told him. How could she have not told him?

If not before, how could she have driven away a week ago without saying a word? Without telling him that she'd given birth to his son?

Every moment they'd spent together had been a deception.

Every breath, every touch, every look, every smile, every laugh—all had been lies.

Because she'd known he had a son and she hadn't told him.

Which brought him back to why she'd told him yesterday.

He knew very little about her, other than that she'd volunteered at CCPO as a nurse, drove him crazy sexually, and lived in Chattanooga.

From what he'd seen of her home, it wasn't fancy or very big, but was clean and well-cared-for. As he'd told her the night before, he'd lived in worse overseas.

Much worse.

Because Chrissie's home was filled with love.

Whatever her reasons in telling him about Joss, she loved their son.

It oozed from the picture-filled walls.

It oozed from the way Chrissie held him even in sleep.

Not that she was asleep, because his gaze suddenly collided with her green one. She studied him and he returned the favor.

She didn't move, just lay there watching him. Her hair was tousled from sleep and he had an immediate flashback to a week ago when he'd awakened next to her. That morning they'd stared into each other's eyes in a very different way.

There had been no hurt, no anger.

He felt both at the moment. Betrayed.

How could she have kept their son from him?

Even if he could understand her not telling him four years ago, why hadn't she told him a week ago?

How could she have had sex with him, spent that much time with him, all the while knowing what she'd done?

What kind of person did that?

Taking care to be quiet, he got up and left the room.

Mainly because the longer he sat, the more upset he got. He paced across to stare at a photo of a baby Joss with a toothy grin.

He sensed Chrissie behind him before he heard her.

Still, he didn't turn, just stared at the photo.

He'd missed so much. "You should have told me."

"We went through this last night. How was I supposed to know you'd want to know?"

He spun to look at her. She still wore her sweats and baggy T-shirt. Her hair went in several different directions. She was beautiful, but all he could think was how much she'd stolen from him.

"He's my son," he reminded her, liking how the words sounded on his tongue. "Why wouldn't I want to know?"

"Not every man does."

"Yeah, well, I'm not every man."

She raked her fingers through her hair. "No, you aren't."

"What's that supposed to mean?"

She flinched. "Can we not do this today?"

"What?"

"I don't want to argue with you, Trace."

"Yeah, well, you should have thought about that before you kept my son from me."

"You know, Trace, that goes two ways?"

"I didn't keep our son from you."

"No, you didn't, but guess what? You didn't come looking for me, either."

"There's a big difference. I didn't know you were pregnant, Chrissie."

Her chin shot up defiantly. "You didn't ask."

"Seriously?" He rounded on her. "A man is supposed to have to ask a woman to find out that she's pregnant?"

She closed her eyes. "Okay, you're right. That didn't make sense. Not really. I—"

"Not at all," he interrupted. "You should have told me and you know it."

"Mommy?"

Both Trace's and Chrissie's heads spun toward the little boy standing in the doorway. He wore superhero pajamas and his fair hair was a little tousled, but his eyes were what got to Trace. He had inherited the Stevens eyes. He'd noticed it in the photos, but in person Joss's eyes were mirror reflections of his own. Of his father's.

"Hey, baby," Chrissie greeted, going over and scooping him into her arms and kissing the top of his head.

The little boy patted her cheek, staring back at Trace with suspicion through eyes identical to his own.

His knees went weak and he reached out to steady himself.

Joss was his.

His son who looked at him and saw a stranger.

A stranger who had been arguing with his mother.

Trace took a deep breath.

Today was going to be difficult because he wanted to take the boy and hug him, to have him hug him back, to have his little hands against his cheek the way he was touching Chrissie.

It wasn't going to happen.

Not without patience.

Trace had learned a lot about patience during his

time overseas, but this might be the hardest thing he'd ever done. Plus, he only had limited time before he'd be gone.

A very limited time.

"Joss," Chrissie said in a soft tone. "This is Mommy's friend."

At her introduction, Trace's jaw worked. Had she thought he was kidding when he said she'd tell the truth?

He'd lost enough time with Joss.

He wouldn't lose more, nor would he have his kid thinking he was just one of Mommy's friends.

Chrissie felt Joss's fingers tangle into her hair, while he continued to stare at Trace. The finger tangling was something he frequently did when overly tired or nervous.

She'd never had any non-related man to their house, so how tightly her son's legs dug into her waist didn't surprise her. He definitely had his reservations about waking up to her arguing with a stranger.

A stranger who desperately didn't want to be a stranger.

Trace's restraint showed in every sinew of his body, which probably didn't reassure Joss.

Her stomach twisted much tighter than Joss's fingers in her hair.

Trace wanted her to tell Joss that he was his father.

She had to tell him, but how did one tell a child that he was looking at a father he didn't know he had?

"Chrissie." Trace stressed her name.

She walked over closer to Trace, causing Joss to cling tighter. No doubt her own nerves were affecting his comfort level, too, but there was nothing she could do about that. No way were her nerves going to settle.

"Joss…" she did her best to keep her voice calm, reassuring, but her insides felt completely the opposite "…Trace is a very special person who is going to stay with us for a while. Can you say hello?"

Her son made a grunting sound and turned his head away from Trace, burying his face against her chest.

Trace's expression was taut, his normally tan skin pale, his eyes watery and desperate for recognition.

Her heart ached with misery for him. She couldn't imagine seeing her child for the first time and him rejecting her when all she wanted to do was love him.

The look in Trace's eyes said he did want to love their son and how she handled the next few minutes would make a major impact on how Joss responded to Trace.

"Joss, do you remember our stories about daddies?" She leaned back, trying to maneuver

Joss to where she could see his face, but he burrowed down farther against her chest. "Well, Trace is your daddy. Isn't that wonderful?"

That got Joss's attention and he mumbled something against her chest that she couldn't make out.

"What was that, baby?"

But whatever Joss had said was lost and he apparently wasn't repeating. Just as well because she thought he had said he didn't want a daddy.

She glanced up at Trace and gave a weak smile, then tried again. "Joss, do you think you could show Trace…um…your daddy your trains? He really likes trains and I bet he'd love to see yours."

"You have trains?" Trace tried, his voice overly eager. "Your mom is right. I love trains."

"Do you like Thomas?" Joss mumbled, still not looking up from his hunkered-against-her position.

Trace looked at her for help.

"Joss, if you'll go show Trace…um…your daddy, your trains, I'll cook us some breakfast. I can make those smiley-face pancakes you like." She tried to keep her voice normal, level, not as if she'd just introduced her son to his father.

But Joss wasn't having any of it.

Trains weren't going to distract him from the fact that there was a strange man in their house and his mommy was full of over-the-top tension.

"Do your trains make noise?" Trace asked, not giving up.

"Can you tell your daddy what your trains say?"

With a shy glance toward Trace, then a return to burying his face into her neck, Joss shook his head. He wasn't an overly shy child, typically, but no doubt the surprise of an unexpected houseguest and the fact they'd been arguing hadn't set the right tone. Trace should have gotten a hotel, let her talk to Joss and ease him into the idea of having a daddy.

Or maybe she should have just told Joss about his dad from the beginning. Or vice versa.

"Can I show him your trains?" she asked, hoping to help break the ice, but Joss shook his head.

"Pancakes."

"Okay," she agreed with her son's one-word response, then glanced at Trace. "Trace, why don't you help me cook breakfast? Joss can help, too. He's a really great helper."

CHAPTER TWELVE

CHRISSIE WASN'T SURE what was running through Joss's head, but he'd not let her out of his sight all day. He didn't have the opportunity to meet many strangers, but she'd not realized quite how clingy he was. Maybe it was that he'd met Trace in such an unusual way within their home and their raised voices had possibly awakened him. Regardless, her son had been superclingy and had wanted to be held more than he had since he'd first learned to walk.

Not that she didn't normally love the opportunity to hold her usually energetic three-year-old fireball, but Joss's clinginess was over exaggerated and breaking her heart for Trace.

They'd stayed in, played trains, watched one of Joss's favorite cartoon movies, and then gone for a walk around her neighborhood, while pushing him in his stroller. She'd made them grilled cheese sandwiches and cut fresh fruit for their lunch. To her surprise Trace had cleaned the kitchen while she'd colored with Joss. When he'd joined them, Joss had given him a suspicious look, but had shared a crayon and one of his books.

She'd tried to sneak away to start a load of laundry, a never-ending job, but Joss followed her into the tiny room off the kitchen where the washer and dryer were located and stayed with her until she'd finished.

She'd cooked dinner, given Joss a bath, read a half-dozen stories, and eventually he'd gone to sleep.

Trace had been right there all day, but Joss hadn't warmed to him despite his great efforts.

It bothered Chrissie a great deal.

Partly because Joss had never responded to anyone in such a guarded way. But mostly, because she knew her son treating his father as a stranger was her fault.

Because she hadn't included him in Joss's life.

She could make a thousand excuses, some of them valid, some of them less so. No excuse changed the truth. It was her fault Joss didn't know and love Trace.

She couldn't make her son warm up to his father, but she could do her best to make sure he didn't pick up on bad vibes from her.

Easier said than done.

She'd fought vibes all day.

Nervous vibes.

Scared-about-her-future vibes.

Attracted-to-a-man-she-was-pretty-sure-hated-her vibes.

How could he not?

She couldn't blame him. Wouldn't she hate someone who had kept such a precious miracle from her?

But how could she have known Trace would want to know Joss?

Duh. That one was easy. She could have known if she'd told him, given him the opportunity to make the choice of whether or not he wanted to be a part of their son's life.

She hadn't.

"I don't know how you get anything done," Trace said when they got back into the living room after Joss was settled in.

"Some days are easier than others," she admitted. "I'm sorry he was standoffish. He'll get used to you and warm up."

"I know," Trace said, but the emotion in his voice gave truth to how affected he'd been. "It's not as if I expected him to start calling me Daddy today."

But the crackle in his voice said he had hoped for it.

What had she done? she wondered, her heart doing a little crackling of its own. How could she ever make up for depriving Trace of the first years of their son's life?

"I'm going to go for a run," he announced.

Surprised by his sudden announcement and disappearance out of her front door, Chrissie stared at the now empty room with a heavy heart.

A heavy heart because she was confused by the emotions battling for dominance within her. Especially the great sense of loss she felt that Trace was no longer in her home.

She did a few of the chores she usually did on her days off work, then showered. When a sweaty Trace came back into the house, she was sitting on the sofa, feet tucked beneath her, reading a book.

That she felt relieved he'd returned made no sense. Of course he'd returned. His SUV was parked in her driveway. Had she thought he'd keep running all the way to Atlanta?

"You okay if I shower now?" His gaze didn't quite meet hers.

"That's fine."

He paused before heading out of the living room. "I'll grab my bag out of your bedroom and take the sofa tonight."

More guilt hit her.

"I don't mind sleeping with Joss again," she offered.

He shook his head. "Nah, I think it would be best if you get back to your normal routine as much as possible."

Maybe he was right.

He turned to go and the need to say something more burned inside her.

"I'm sorry, Trace."

If not for the slightest pause in his step she'd have thought he didn't hear her. But his steps had paused, then resumed without his acknowledging her apology.

Chrissie let out a long sigh.

What a mess she'd made.

Three days had passed since Trace's arrival and Chrissie would return to work the following morning. They'd decided to go to the aquarium on her last day off before she pulled another five twelve-hour shifts in a row.

Although Trace had been with them almost non-stop over the past three days, Joss hadn't warmed to him.

Typically, Joss was a people person and a natural-born charmer, like his father, but with Trace he was standoffish and almost cruel in how he refused to interact.

For the most part, Trace remained patient and just kept trying, but his frustration was palpable.

Maybe that was what Joss sensed that kept him from interacting with or freely smiling at Trace.

"I'm excited to see the penguins, Joss," Trace said as he attempted to get Joss out of his car seat. To no avail. Joss stubbornly insisted upon Chrissie unbuckling him and holding his hand as he jumped from the car onto the hot pavement.

Once on the pavement, he ignored Trace's outstretched hand and kept a death grip on Chrissie's.

Trace's look her way was full of pure disgust.

This was her fault, his eyes said. She'd done this. Guilt filled her. She deserved his scorn.

Then again, who would have thought Joss would

react so negatively? Because her son's reaction to his father was beyond anything she could have imagined from her sweet little boy.

Joss intentionally tried to exclude Trace more often than not. Just as he was currently doing, ignoring Trace and tugging on her hand.

"Can I get in the water?"

Ahead of them there was a small artsy-looking fountain just below a warped rainbow-shaped bridge walkway where several children were splashing.

"Maybe after we see the penguins," she told him with a gentle tone. "Your daddy is excited to see them. Do you think he'll like the manta rays, too?"

Joss loved the aquarium and especially the exhibit where visitors could reach into the water and "pet" manta rays that passed by. She'd bought them an annual pass earlier in the year and, though they'd been several times, his fascination with the aquatic life had never waned.

Until today.

"I don't want to see the manta rays." Joss's lower lip hung low. "I want to play in the water."

Good grief. Trace probably thought Joss was a spoiled brat. Hopefully he'd take into account that the child had just had his entire world turned upside down with meeting his father.

Still, she didn't want to encourage his behavior.

"After we go inside to show your daddy the penguins," she repeated with what she hoped was the right combination of gentleness and sternness. "If you be good."

Joss's gaze, so similar to Trace's, took on a steely stubbornness. "He can go by himself. We don't want him here."

Trace winced.

Chrissie let out a frustrated sigh. "Of course we want your daddy here. We want to show him the penguins and let him pet the manta rays."

Joss gave her a look that said she could verbalize whatever she wanted, but he wasn't buying it.

Trace didn't look as if he was either.

Then again, as much as Trace was trying, maybe he was trying too hard, and scowling too much when he failed. Maybe that was why Joss wouldn't relax.

Or maybe her smart little three-year-old was still picking up on his mother's nervousness.

Trace bought his ticket, then they waited in line to enter the aquarium. Within a few minutes they were riding the long escalator up to the top.

"Do you think the otters will be playing today?" she asked Joss, hoping to distract him out of his sour mood.

The little boy's eyes lit with interest, but then he seemed to recall that he wasn't happy with his mother or life in general.

Frustrated with Joss's behavior but afraid she'd just make things worse by scolding him, plus knowing it couldn't be easy on him to have unexpectedly had Trace move in with them three days ago, Chrissie turned to Trace. She'd caused this tension. It was up to her to break the ice.

"These cute little otters live at the top of the aquarium. Sometimes when we visit, they are sleeping and sometimes they are playing." She injected as much perkiness as she could muster. "We like when they are playing, don't we, Joss?"

Joss didn't answer.

Chrissie kept right on talking as if all were wonderful. Not that she felt wonderful. Not that Trace looked as if he was having a good time. Certainly, Joss seemed determined not to enjoy himself.

Fine. She could do this. She'd dealt with worse situations. At least, she thought she had, even if she couldn't think of any.

The otters were playing and that went a long way to lightening Joss's mood. When one swam near the thick glass wall that allowed seeing his underwater antics, Joss's eyes grew big.

"Look," he exclaimed, pointing excitedly.

"I think he likes you," Chrissie praised when the otter seemed to be checking Joss out as much as the little boy was checking out him.

"He probably recognizes me from when I came before."

"Maybe so." She turned to Trace. "Cute, huh?"

His gaze met hers and something flickered that put an entirely different nervous energy in her belly.

"Adorable," he said, bending to Joss's level to eye the otter next to their son.

After watching the otters for a while longer, they slowly made their way through the different exhibits.

They hung out in the butterfly area for a while. A large monarch landed on Trace's finger.

"Look," Trace breathed in an excited whisper, as if he was afraid if he made too much noise the butterfly would take flight.

"It's beautiful," Chrissie said.

The butterfly seemed to have taken up residence on Trace's finger, not minding one bit when Trace knelt and offered the butterfly to Joss.

The boy regarded the butterfly with longing. "Do you think he'll fly off if I hold him?"

"Only one way to find out." Trace gently transferred the butterfly to Joss's stretched-out finger.

Chrissie held her breath during the transfer, praying the butterfly cooperated, and amazingly it did, resting on Joss's finger while he did his best to keep his hand still.

A proud Joss looked up at her and grinned. "Take my picture."

Heart melting, Chrissie got out her cell phone and snapped a couple of shots of Joss holding the butterfly. Trace stood to the side watching.

"Step in behind Joss so I can get your picture with him and the butterfly," she suggested, elated when Trace complied. A little dazed, too, at the thought she was about to take a photo of her son with his father.

With shaky hands, she snapped several pictures of a smiling Joss holding a butterfly and a smiling Trace standing behind him with his hand on Joss's shoulder. No matter what happened, she'd treasure the photos and believed someday Joss would, too.

Sharing his butterfly must have won Trace more than a few brownie points because Joss lost his scowl for the rest of the morning. He still wouldn't hold Trace's hand but at least he was showing some of his normal enthusiasm for the trip and had become talkative, telling Trace about the different exhibits.

"I don't see the alligator," Trace said, scratching his head and pretending not to see the alligator that was beneath the water in a river exhibit.

"Right there." Joss pointed against the glass in the direction the alligator rested.

Trace bent down to Joss's level. "Where?"

"Right there." Joss tapped the thick clear wall separating the viewing area from the exhibit. "You have to see him. He's huge."

"Now I see him. Thank you," he told the little boy as he looked in the right direction. "I'd hate to have missed seeing him."

"He has big teeth," Joss pointed out, even though you couldn't see much as the alligator's mouth was closed.

"The better to eat me with," Trace teased, chomping his teeth.

"Trace," Savannah laughed.

"What? I'm just pointing that out. Just in case."

"Just in case what?"

His expression suggested that maybe he thought she might push him in—not that she could. The glass wall was too high for that.

Not that she'd thought of doing such a thing, anyway.

At least not now that both of her guys were finally smiling.

They continued their trek through the aquarium, going down one floor at a time, petted the manta rays, which Joss loved, then finished up their tour at the souvenir shop.

"Can I have a toy, Mommy, please?"

"Not today, Joss. We bought the stuffed penguin the last time we were here and I told you we wouldn't get anything the next time we came."

"But I need a manta ray."

Yeah, her sweet little angel was on a roll.

"Not today."

"Why not?"

The question had come from Trace and had both Chrissie and Joss looking his way.

Chrissie didn't want to argue with him, especially not in front of Joss. She forced a smile. "Because Joss got a toy the last time he came and we don't get new toys every time. He knows that."

She didn't want Joss to grow up spoiled and unappreciative of life's blessings. She tried to find a balance and for the most part felt she succeeded. Her son knew they didn't get new souvenirs at every visit.

Trace bent to Joss's level. "If you want the manta ray, I'll buy it for you. An otter, too, if you want it."

Joss's eyes immediately went to hers. If she'd already told him no on something, she didn't allow others to then do it for him. At three, he already knew this, although he wasn't beyond trying on occasion with his grandmother.

Trying to choose her words carefully, Chrissie started to explain to Trace that she'd already said no and that was the end of it. Because she had final say. Because she was the parent.

But so was Trace.

That was when the full ramifications of Trace being in their lives hit her.

She no longer had final say over decisions where Joss was concerned. She no longer got to decide what was good for him and what was bad for him and how much was just right. At least, not by herself she didn't get to decide those things.

If he wanted to buy Joss the entire store, he had just as much right to do that as she had to say no.

What if she and Trace fundamentally disagreed on even the most basic of things when it came to child rearing?

What if they never agreed and one always said

no and the other always said yes? What if Joss grew to hate her because she was the parent who tried to create boundaries and Trace showered him with gifts?

What if Joss treated her the way he treated Trace?

Her skin began to shrink around her body, squeezing her insides to where she felt as if she were about to cave in on herself. To where every breath was a struggle.

Her gaze met Trace's and she tried to speak, but nothing came out. Nothing.

Panic rising in her throat, she glanced around the shop, her mind racing, her feet itching, her knees weak.

"No—just no." With that, she grabbed Joss's hand and walked over to a shark book display and fought the paralysis taking hold of her body.

Because she wanted to run, with Joss, and never turn back.

But she wasn't like her father. No matter how strong that urge inside her was, she knew she wasn't.

Not quite understanding what had just happened, Trace watched Chrissie practically freeze next to a book display.

His gaze dropped down to where Chrissie clinched Joss's little hand in a death grip.

Obviously confused, Joss kept turning to look at him expectantly, waiting for him to respond.

Because he was the adult here. Not that he had any clue what had just happened.

He wanted to give Joss things, for Joss to have something physical that he'd given him. A stuffed manta ray was as good a place to start as any.

"I'll get the manta ray and meet you two out front," he offered.

"Fine," Chrissie agreed, keeping her back to him.

Too bad, because he'd really like to see what was in those expressive eyes of hers right now.

Joss was looking at him though. And not in a good way. His little face squished up, his eyes watered, then he shook his head. "I don't need a manta ray."

His tone sounded almost identical to what Chrissie's had earlier, only with a big heap of sadness.

Good grief. More was going on here than whether or not a stuffed toy was going to be bought. Way more. Not that Trace understood what was running through Chrissie's head, but something sure was.

"I'd like to buy you one, but if you want to wait until next time, we can."

The tears welling in his eyes threatened to spill down his cheeks. "Can we go home?"

All kinds of heartstrings were pulling in dozens of directions as he looked into his son's sorrowful eyes.

"Yes, we can."

Only Joss had to go to the bathroom. When Chrissie started to take him into the women's room, which was what he guessed she usually did rather than let Joss go into a bathroom alone, Trace had to speak up.

"I'll take him with me into the men's room."

Fear lit her eyes. Real, no-holds-barred fear. Which confused Trace every bit as much as her behavior over his buying the kid a stuffed manta ray.

"It's really no bother," she protested. "It's what we usually do."

"Chrissie, it's ridiculous for him to go into the ladies' room when I'm right here and can take him to the men's room."

"But…"

He watched the very real struggle on her face, watched the physical effort she had to exert for her to let go of the boy's hand.

"Okay. I'll be waiting." She glanced around, through the glass. "There. On that bench. I'll be waiting right there. Don't take too long. Please."

Trace really wanted to question her on the stress in her voice. It was only a trip to the bathroom. Was it a trust thing? Did she think he wouldn't keep an eye on their son? That he'd scold him if he had an accident? That he'd forget to make him wash his hands? What?

Although Chrissie's saying no had robbed him of the chance of giving his son a present, Joss's need for the bathroom had given him the gift of holding Joss's hand without the boy pulling away, whether that was out of courtesy or out of knowledge that they were in a public place and he needed to be holding an adult's hand. Either way, Trace was grateful for the tiny hand clasped inside his.

Trace stayed right with Joss, talked to him, and was proud of the way the three-year-old, who was in such a hurry to get back to his mother, managed himself in the bathroom, including automatically wanting to wash his hands afterward. Chrissie had taught their son well.

When they exited the bathroom, Joss spotted Chrissie immediately, even prior to Trace doing so.

"There she is!" he called, sounding relieved she was there. Had he thought she was leaving them despite her saying she'd be waiting?

Then again, the relief on Chrissie's face at spotting them had Trace pausing. What the…?

Joss pulled on Trace's hand, wanting to dash toward where Chrissie sat on a bench close to where the water was that Joss had wanted to get into earlier.

"Slow down, son," Trace told him, falling back into step with his son. "We're headed that way."

But Joss kept on tugging, setting as fast a pace as possible to his mother.

When they joined her, Chrissie looked up, her gaze searching them both, as if looking for battle scars.

She glanced toward the water. "Do you still want to play in the water?"

But rather than answer immediately, Joss studied her face, trying to gauge her expression on what she wanted him to say, as if he wasn't quite sure how to take her odd behavior in the aquarium shop.

Which irked Trace. Was she emotionally manipulating their son because he'd spoken up to buy the boy something she'd said no to? Did the fact Joss had lightened up to him a little bother her and she wanted to add the tension back?

He hadn't thought she was trying to prevent Joss from warming to him, but maybe she was.

"I'd like to play in the water," Chrissie added, smiling at her son, albeit a little weakly. "And I bet your daddy would like to play in the water, too."

Okay, so maybe he was being paranoid. Or letting his frustration over her having rushed out of the souvenir shop mess with his head. Or maybe everything these days was messing with his head.

Joss and his reluctance to have much to do with him. Chrissie and his mixed-up feelings for her. Physically, he wanted her and ached for her. Emotionally, he'd never felt more betrayed.

Joss glanced up at Trace with big, uncertain eyes. "Would you?"

Oh, heaven of heavens.

"I would."

More than anything in the world he'd like to play in the water with this little boy.

And his mother.

Chrissie left the bench and went to the pool of water. She sat on the edge, obviously not caring that her shorts were likely to have damp spots when she stood. She slipped her sandals off and put her feet into the water.

"That's cold," she said, wrapping her arms around her chest and pretending to shiver despite the hot sun.

Relaxing, Joss laughed and joined her, quickly stripping off his own shoes.

"Brr..." he said as he stepped into the water and wrapped his little arms around himself. "It is cold."

"Unless you're a penguin," Chrissie added, sending a tiny splash her son's way. "And then it's just right."

"I'm a penguin," Joss said, a big smile on his face, as if all was perfect in his world and always had been. "A big ole penguin looking for a fish to eat."

He made a chomping motion.

Finally relaxing, too, Chrissie laughed.

Trace watched in amazement at how quickly Joss had gone from pouty to remorseful to carefree as he pranced around in the water that came up to the edge of his shorts. Each exaggerated step he took splashed water all around him, but not nearly so much as when he smacked the water with his little hands and burst into giggles.

"Daddy," Chrissie called, sending a spray of water in Trace's direction. "You afraid this penguin is going to mistake you for a big juicy fish?"

Joss made a chomping noise toward Trace, seeming okay that Chrissie had included him in their fun.

"Nah, we penguins can tell other penguins apart from big juicy fish quite easily." He kicked off his shoes, stepped into the water, and made a chomping noise that was a decent imitation of the sounds Joss was making.

"Mommy is a big juicy fish," Joss declared, heading her way, and giggling when Trace did the same. "We're going to get you, fishy-fishy."

"Are you a hungry penguin?" she teased when Trace got close.

"Very hungry." He made another chomping sound and Joss squealed, half in delight and half in possible concern.

"Don't really eat her. She's my mommy."

"Good point," Trace agreed, his eyes still locked with Chrissie's, trying to read what had triggered her mood change.

If it hadn't been an intentional attempt to keep emotional distance between him and Joss, and he had to admit to himself that, up to that point, she'd gone above and beyond in trying to get Joss to warm to him, then what?

Whatever it had been, she seemed determined to keep a smile on her face now.

Or on Joss's at any rate, because their son burst into excited squeals when Chrissie splashed Trace with water again.

"That does it. You're mine, fishy-fishy," he warned, calling her by the same name as Joss had used.

"Nope, she's mine," Joss corrected, splashing over to where Chrissie was and pretending to gobble her up. "Mmm… She tastes good."

At which Trace's mind took off in a completely non-innocent way as his gaze met hers.

"Yeah, she does."

Chrissie's eyes darkened. His gut tightened.

Without a doubt, he knew he should have kept that thought to himself because the last thing he needed was to complicate things further by becoming involved physically with Chrissie again.

CHAPTER THIRTEEN

"TODAY WAS A better day," Chrissie mused that evening as she and Trace slipped out of Joss's bedroom.

They'd bathed him, read to him, and put him to bed quite some time ago. Joss had been a bit wound up and it had taken a good thirty minutes to get him settled. She'd tried to let Trace read to him, but Joss had insisted she read his stories. Even so, Joss hadn't been opposed to Trace being in the room, listening to the stories. Instead of the resentment from the previous nights, he'd instead cast his gaze at his father during the "good' parts, as if gauging Trace's reaction.

Eventually he'd dozed off to sleep.

Trace didn't respond to her comment until they were in the living room. His question felt more like an attack.

"Why didn't you let him have a manta ray?"

"What?" she asked, sitting on the far end of the sofa. His question caught her off guard. Mainly, because the rest of their day had been fairly good, considering. Joss hadn't been so standoffish and Chrissie had managed not to break down at the thought that Trace had just as much say in the raising of their son as she did, that he had just as much right to their son as she did.

Even now the thought just felt wrong.

"You heard me," Trace pointed out, taking the other end of the sofa. "What was the big deal about him getting a stuffed animal? He should be able to have a keepsake from the first time he went to the aquarium with me."

When he put it that way…

"Sorry." She really was. About so many things. Like her irrational fear that Trace might have taken off with Joss when she'd left them alone. "I wasn't thinking about it being the first time he went with you when I said no. I don't want him spoiled and had told him the last time we were there that if he got something that day, that he wouldn't be able to the next time he came."

Trace crossed his arms and stared at her from the other end of the sofa. His scowl didn't relent. "Okay, so you were going for consistency in your parenting. I understand that. But maybe you'd like to explain what was such a big deal about me taking him to the bathroom?"

"No, I wouldn't like to explain that." Because how petty did it sound that she'd panicked at the thought that she no longer had final say over her son, but now shared that responsibility with Trace? That she'd been afraid he might take off with their son if she left them alone? Trace had given her no reason to think he'd do that, so pretty petty.

The deepening furrow of his brows warned he wasn't going to let her answer ride.

A damn burst inside her and emotions came gushing forward full-force.

"You're not the only one dealing with a lot of new, mixed emotions, you know," she blurted out, surprising both her and Trace with her intensity. "I wasn't expecting you to come here and demand to stay at my house and interrupt our lives."

His brow lifted. "You thought I'd stay away after your phone call?"

"I didn't know what to think. You were the one who said you didn't want children. Four years ago and less than two weeks ago. Plus, you're leaving the country again soon. When I called I thought you might already have gone."

"And yet you called."

He made it sound like a dirty thing that she had done. Did he wish he could go back to not knowing Joss existed?

"You don't have to be here. Just go back to Atlanta or wherever it is you'd rather be. There's nothing Joss and I need from you."

"No, you've done a really good job convincing my son that he doesn't need a father."

"Of course I have. I want him to grow up happy and healthy and if he bemoaned the fact that he didn't have a father it might affect his mental and emotional health." Didn't she know firsthand how growing up without a father felt? "I'd never knowingly let that happen."

"But you would have allowed him to grow up

without a father had our paths not crossed again at CCPO?"

"Probably," she admitted, hating that it was true, but acknowledging it all the same. "I'd convinced myself I was doing you a favor in not telling you."

"Because?"

"Because I thought you were living the high life in Atlanta…that you didn't want to be tied down by a relationship and kids." She tossed his former claim back at him.

"And what is it you want, Chrissie? What is it you hope to gain from having told me about Joss?"

He had money and was probably implying that was why she'd told him. If so, he was wrong.

"There isn't a thing you have that I want," she declared with a tilt of her chin.

Her angry spark had his brow arching.

"Isn't there?"

She shook her head.

"We both know that if I touched you, you'd go up in smoke."

No, she didn't know that. Well, maybe she did, but she wasn't admitting to a thing.

"If you think I haven't noticed how you watch me, you're wrong."

Okay, so maybe she watched him. A lot.

"You're a man living in my house uninvited. Of course I watch you. Trying to make sure you don't steal the silverware."

"Ha," he snorted. "Real funny."

"Despite your claims of wealth, I know nothing about you, Trace. Nothing. So don't you go making fun of me trying to protect my son and myself."

He considered her answer a moment, then said, "You know all you've asked to find out."

"Fine. Since you keep bringing him up, tell me about your father."

"I don't talk about my dad."

Yeah, neither did she, but still, she tossed her hands up in frustration. "Exactly my point. You say one thing and do another. Just as I asked you to tell me what happened to your side and you didn't."

The struggle on his face was real. "What is it you want to know about my father?"

"Why don't you get along with him?" She could tell that her question wasn't one he'd been expecting or that he wanted to answer. The struggle intensified.

"Because he's a wealthy businessman who thinks he can control everyone and everything if he waves around enough money."

"Can he?"

"What?"

"Control everyone and everything with money?"

Trace shrugged. "Just about."

"But not you?"

"No."

A lot of things began to click in her mind. "He's why you went overseas?"

"No," he immediately denied.

But she knew the real reason was probably yes. They sat in silence a moment.

"What are your intentions, Trace?"

"Regarding you? I have no intentions. I don't do relationships or marriage."

"Not in regards to me." Why would he think she was even asking that? Because of his off-the-wall comment in the wading pool? "In regards to Joss. What are you going to do?"

"I'm going to stay with him tomorrow to watch him while you go to work."

She fought grimacing. "I don't think that's a good idea. My mother is planning to watch him. She said she'd come here about ten—that way you could still spend time with Joss, but she'd be here to help."

She had called her mother and told her only the basics. When she'd begun asking questions, Chrissie had promised she'd call her at break the following day and fill her in.

"I do think it's a good idea. He and I need time to bond."

Which came back to that shared power over their son. There she went thinking she got final say, rather than sharing the responsibility with Trace. Guilt and remorse were powerful motivators, but she still couldn't agree with him.

"Do you think you're ready to be alone with Joss all day? There's a lot to taking care of him, Trace."

"I've been with him for four days, Chrissie. I

won't claim to have your vast experience with parenting, but I'm a grown man, lived in war-torn countries, and a medical doctor. I think I'll survive a day alone with my three-year-old son. I don't need your mother to babysit us both."

His barb regarding her having excluded him from gaining parenting experience wasn't lost.

She grabbed a sofa pillow and hugged it to her. "Yeah, it's not you I was worried about."

His gaze narrowed. "You think I'd hurt my son?"

"Not intentionally."

"Which means what?

"That I think you want him to like you so much that it blinds you to being able to think logically around him like a real parent."

She regretted her word choice the moment it left her mouth, but couldn't take the "real" back no matter how much she wished she could.

His face darkened to an angry red. "I'd say it's normal for a father to want his son to like him, to be his friend."

"It's not your job to be his friend, Trace. You're a parent, not a bestie."

"I'm not sure I even know what you mean by that."

"Which just proves my point."

"You'll have to excuse me. I've only been a parent for four days. Nature didn't notify me of my pending parenthood four years ago and neither did my son's mother."

He got up and went to the front door. "I'm going for a run, but I will be back and I will watch my son tomorrow. Leave me written instructions on anything you think is vital I know that a 'real' father would know about their son."

With those sharp emotional digs, he stormed out of the front door and was gone.

Ha. It would serve him right if she locked him out of the house.

Not that she would, but the thought made her feel a little better.

But not much.

With sleeping on Chrissie's sofa, not waking up as she moved around the house in preparation for leaving for work was impossible.

Trace had always been a light sleeper, but, since his time overseas, he often felt he slept with one eye open and one ear on guard.

Not one for pretense, he sat up and was stretching when Chrissie entered the room.

Her gaze immediately went to his bare chest and a rosy blush stained her cheeks.

"Um…" she muttered, stopping in her tracks and not seeming to know what to say.

Trace glanced down at his bare chest. "Something wrong?"

"You shouldn't sleep half naked."

He laughed. "I'm wearing shorts, Chrissie."

Her gaze went back to his chest, then jerked away. "Whatever."

"Does my lack of shirt bother you?"

"Yes."

"Why?"

"You know why," she snapped.

Excitement rushed through him. "You like what you see?"

"You know you're a beautiful man. You don't need forced compliments from me."

Only maybe he did because her words pleased him more than they should have.

"My scar doesn't bother you? You mentioned it yesterday. Some women would find it ugly."

Her gaze dropped to where his shorts rode low, revealing the edge of his puckered skin. The pink to her cheeks turned ashen and he wondered what she thought.

"How I find you doesn't matter, Trace. What matters is that you take care of our son today. My mom will be here not too long after Joss wakes."

He sighed. She was right.

"You have my cell-phone number," she reminded him, determined to be all business. "I've written down my mother's number and my friend Savannah's number in case you need anything before Mom gets here. I left the paper on the kitchen countertop. If you can't reach me, call either of them."

"It's ridiculous for you to have your mother come here. I've got this."

"But she will be here. Promise you'll call if you need anything," she insisted.

"If I run into problems, I'll call." He stood, noting that her gaze followed the descent of the blanket as it dropped to the floor, then her eyes traced back up to meet his.

How his body could respond to her when he was so aggravated at her lack of confidence in him, he wasn't sure, but, same as always, his body responded.

"Um…that's good," she muttered, dragging her gaze away.

Trace stepped from the sofa, yawning, then raking his fingers through his hair. "Yeah, but Joss and I are going to have a good day, despite having your mom looking over my shoulder, so I won't be calling."

He was still telling himself that an hour later when Joss refused to eat. He'd awakened earlier than Chrissie had thought he would as it was still almost an hour before her mother would arrive. After a while of cajoling him, answering Chrissie's second text asking how things were going, Trace decided Joss would eat when hunger hit him.

But when the boy started crying for his mother and Trace couldn't get him to stop, he realized he was going to have to get them out of the house so he could distract him from Chrissie's absence. Ei-

ther that or have her mother walk into the house with Joss upset. Then Chrissie really wouldn't trust him with their son.

"Joss, before you woke up this morning, I was researching some of the things we could do. I'd like to go to the train station to ride in a train. Would you like that?"

Joss didn't look overly excited. "I like trains."

Not that liking trains improved his flat-tire attitude much. Every movement seemed to be a chore. Joss complained of his stomach hurting and still refused to eat.

Trace let out a big sigh and went in search of the bag Chrissie had brought with them each time they'd left the house. A bag from which she'd magically pulled out anything Joss had needed when they'd been away from her home.

He searched through the bag, checking contents, doing his best to figure out what might be missing from what Chrissie packed. He grabbed a couple of juice boxes from the fridge, and filled a plastic container of dry cereal. He shouldn't need more than that as he'd buy his and Joss's lunch at The Chattanooga Choo-Choo hotel where the train would leave from.

He'd buy anything else he might have forgotten.

He'd gone the night before and bought a car seat so he and Joss wouldn't be trapped at the house all day. No doubt, Chrissie wouldn't want him going anywhere with their son as she hadn't mentioned

leaving a seat for him to use and surely she knew he wouldn't have taken his son out without a seat. Joss's safety and well-being was everything. On that, he and Chrissie agreed.

Unfortunately, Joss seemed back into his uncooperative state and sat down in the gravel, saying he wanted his mommy, while Trace figured out how to securely fasten the car seat into the back seat of his SUV.

"Your mommy is at work, but she will be home this evening." Patience, he reminded himself. He had to be patient. Joss would grow to love him, too. Would eventually accept him as his father. Maybe not before he had to leave, though. "You and I are going to go ride a train and have some boy fun."

"I don't want to have boy fun," his son whined. "I want Mommy."

Yeah, Trace didn't blame him. Given the option of hanging with Chrissie or himself, he'd choose Chrissie, too.

"Mommy is at work," he repeated. "You and I are going on an adventure. It'll be great," Trace assured him. Definitely more fun than them staying home and him trying to figure out what to do all day long with Chrissie's mother casting a critical eye. What had she even told her mother about him? Had she been honest and admitted that Trace hadn't known about Joss or was he the villain in her eyes? "Your mom will be home tonight when she gets off work."

In the meantime, he wanted to bond with Joss and believed their being alone was the best way of achieving that. He'd shoot Chrissie's mother a text once they reached the Choo-Choo.

"My stomach hurts," Joss complained.

Trace sighed. Today would get better, just as it had at the aquarium. He and Joss would have a good time. Once he got Joss to the trains, he'd get excited about their trip. This would be a good day.

"I brought you some juice and cereal. I'll give it to you once I get you fastened into your car seat."

Was Joss allowed to eat while in his car seat? Surely. He was three years old and fed himself his meals and snacks.

Trace battled getting the car-seat strap properly fitted through the appropriate part of the car seat. Joss watched him conquer the car seat, but didn't look nearly as impressed as Trace felt he should.

He picked Joss up and put him in the seat, letting Joss help him fasten the seat's buckle into place.

"Great job," he praised, hoping for a smile.

Looking quite miserable, Joss asked, "Can I have my juice?"

Counting to ten, Trace dug into the bag and pulled out one of the juice boxes. "Here ya go, pal."

Joss took the juice box, staring at it expectantly, then back up at Trace. Did Chrissie open the boxes? He hadn't noticed her doing so, but Joss was waiting for him to do something and putting the straw in seemed the most likely.

"Can I get that for you?" he asked, not wanting to offend if he was misreading his son.

Joss nodded, then shook his head. "I'm not thirsty now."

Trace wasn't going to argue. He took the box and put it back into the insulated side pocket of the bag. "Fine. You can have it later."

He wanted to take the top off his car, but decided he'd save that for another day. A day when Joss was showing a little more excitement regarding riding with him. Today, the boy looked two steps away from crying.

He probably was.

He'd asked for Chrissie more than a dozen times and had looked devastated when he'd realized she had gone to work and left him alone with Trace.

He'd even asked about going to his nanna's and had looked disappointed when Trace had said they'd be spending the day together and would see his nanna later that afternoon.

Apparently, despite the gains made the previous day, Trace still wasn't worthy of spending the day alone with.

Maybe that was to be expected. He was still essentially a stranger and Joss wasn't used to staying with him. No problem. They were going to have a great first father-son day. They had to start somewhere and that somewhere was today.

Only Joss didn't seem as eager to get things going.

Nor did he want to walk when Trace got him out of the car at the hotel where he'd buy the tickets for their train ride.

"Fine, I'll carry you." After all, that was what Chrissie had done when the boy had clung to her. He'd enjoy a little Joss clinging to him.

Not that Joss planned to give him the opportunity.

"I don't want you to carry me. I want to go home."

"We're going to ride the train, then we'll get some lunch, then, if you still want to go home—" and he hoped the boy wasn't in a rush by that time "—then we'll go home."

Looking on the verge of crying, Joss let his lower lip droop. "My belly hurts."

Lord, help me, Trace prayed. *Help me do and say the right things to make this child trust me and care for me.*

"That's what happens when you don't eat," Trace reminded him gently. "Would you like some of your juice and cereal now while I buy our tickets? You'll feel better after you eat something."

Joss looked hesitant, but nodded. Trace dug out a juice box and container of dry cereal and handed them to his son.

Joss stared up at him in confusion.

Oh, yeah, he needed to pop the straw into the juice box. He did so, then handed it back to his son.

Joss frowned, handed him the container of

cereal back, then took the juice container with both hands.

After he'd taken a drink, he handed the juice box back to Trace.

"Thank you," the boy said, wiping the back of his hand across his mouth.

Trace took the drink box. Which left the bag draped over Trace's shoulder and the juice box and cereal in his hands. He dropped the cereal back into the bag, held onto the juice, then reached for Joss.

He'd text Chrissie's mother in a few, after they got the tickets.

"You want me to carry you?" he offered, hoping his eagerness didn't come through to the point of scaring Joss.

Joss's lower lip disappeared between his teeth and he shook his head.

Trace would have been better off carrying the boy though, because Joss moved at the slowest speed Trace had ever seen him move. He kept a hold on Joss's hand and tried not to say too much when Joss wriggled.

Tried to focus on the fact that, although Joss wouldn't let him carry him, the boy was holding his hand, something he wouldn't do just a few days ago.

Besides, they still had a good thirty minutes to explore the trains before theirs took off so what did it matter if they took a little longer getting their tickets?

Things went downhill fast once they were actually on the train and moving, though.

Joss began to cry, repeatedly asking for Chrissie. No doubt the other passengers wondered if he was some pervert having kidnapped Joss as he refused to be consoled.

"Joss, we'll go see your mommy when we're through with the train ride."

Joss's tears didn't let up and his little body shook with his distress.

Trace shouldn't have been surprised when the juice Joss had drunk came back up, splattering over the hem of Trace's T-shirt, soaking his shorts, and running down his legs and splattering onto Joss's T-shirt and shorts as well.

Good grief. He hadn't realized Joss had drunk that much of the juice.

Joss's little face looked horrified at what he'd done, almost fearful of how Trace was going to react as his gaze lifted.

Protectiveness surged through him, making him want to hug the boy to him and reassure him.

"It's okay, buddy. You threw up because you got so upset crying. Try to calm down. I'll get you and this mess cleaned up. No big deal." He had the package of wipes in the bag, plus he'd seen a change of clothes in the bag when he'd rummaged through it that morning.

Joss sucked in a sobbing breath, the tears still flowing.

"Shh, it's going to be okay," Trace repeated, gently touching his son's face in hopes of comforting him.

His skin felt on fire and a cold, cold fear gripped Trace.

One that the last time he recalled feeling was when a bomb had gone off and he'd awakened from a nightmare where coworkers and innocent people had senselessly died and many more, including himself, had been injured.

Joss grabbed hold of his right lower abdomen and cried out as if in intense pain.

Please let me be wrong. Please.

He didn't want his son ill. He didn't want to explain to Chrissie how he'd misread everything their son had done that morning and ignored that Joss had appendicitis.

Dear God, please don't let someone else he loved die on his watch.

"You thought I wouldn't stop by the hospital when you're finally not with him so we can talk?" Savannah gave Chrissie a *duh* look.

Chrissie blinked at her best friend. She'd clocked out and gone on break after her friend had shown up in the CVICU. They'd gone down to the hospital cafeteria. It was early, but Chrissie had grabbed a yogurt as she'd take this as her break. Thank goodness the unit was slow that morning so she could escape for a little while with Savannah.

Or maybe not so good as her friend's expression warned she wanted every minute detail of the previous four days. She'd already called her mother, who was running a little late as Chrissie had caught her on her way out of her house, and given her the five-minute study-guide version.

"Um…no, I didn't think you'd show up at work today. Would serve you right if I had you clock in and work the rest of the day," she half teased. Part of her would like to beg her friend to cover the rest of her shift so Chrissie could leave and check on Trace and Joss. They were fine, of course. She was just being an overprotective mom. Besides, her mother would be with them soon. "Does Charlie have Amelia?"

Savannah nodded. "He's watching her while I go to the grocery store and run errands. He says I need to be sure to take 'me' time."

See—Savannah trusted Charlie with Amelia. A dad watching their child was perfectly normal. So why had Chrissie's gut been cramping all morning?

"Confronting me at work falls under the category of 'me' time?"

Savannah shrugged. "Better than me showing up at your house with him there and wanting to know all the juicy details."

"Agreed. Then again, if you wanted to pop by

unexpectedly and check on him and Joss after you leave here, that would be fine by me."

Not that she didn't think they'd be fine. They would be. So why was she so nervous?

"You have to give him credit for being willing to watch Joss. Not all men would have volunteered for that so soon. That he wants to be an active part of Joss's life is a good thing."

"Joss isn't used to him, though."

"Joss is going to have to spend time with him to get used to him, Chrissie. Maybe it's better if you aren't there to run interference so they can get to know each other on their own terms. I hope your mom gives them some space."

"He's leaving the country in a matter of days." Chrissie frowned. "Besides, whose side are you on?"

Savannah's brow rose. "Is this a matter of choosing sides? You should want Joss to be close to his dad."

A dart of guilt pierced her. "He'll be leaving again soon," she repeated. "But, you're right. They need to spend as much time together as possible. I do want that, but…"

She did.

"But you're scared and feel your relationship with your son is threatened by his very presence?"

"If I agreed, that would make me a terrible person and mother, wouldn't it?"

"Or maybe it just means you're human with normal fears and worries?"

Chrissie's head felt heavy and she let her chin fall toward her chest. "He hates me."

"Trace?"

She nodded, wishing she hadn't eaten the yogurt as it felt thick and putrid in her stomach.

"He told you that?"

"No, but I see it in how he looks at me sometimes." How he'd teased her that morning flashed through her mind and her cheeks flushed. That hadn't been hate, but the chemistry between them didn't make anything better. If anything it just added to the confusion.

"That blush tells me that's not the only way he looks at you."

"We have always had phenomenal chemistry," she admitted, not for the first time.

"You're sleeping with him?" Savannah sounded hopeful.

Chrissie shook her head. "He's not so much as kissed me since showing up at my house."

"But you want him to do much more than that?"

She sighed. "It's no secret I find him attractive." Remembering how he'd looked stretching that morning without his shirt made her think she was way underplaying how Trace affected her. She'd not been able to look at him because looking made her want.

"Then why aren't you kissing him?"

Chrissie met her friend's gaze. "What?"

"You said he hadn't so much as kissed you. What about you? Have you kissed him?"

"No, of course not."

Savannah's gaze was piercing. "My question is why not?"

"Everything is so complicated. Sex would just make it more so."

"How?"

"I'd think that was obvious."

"Well, it's not. How would sex make things more complicated? If you ask me, sex might make things better."

"That's because the man you have sex with loves you," she pointed out.

"Trace doesn't love you?"

"No," she answered, but clamped her mouth shut before her next thought came rolling off her tongue, because it couldn't be true.

She didn't wish Trace loved her.

To wish that would make her have to question why she'd wish for such a silly thing. Especially when she knew he hated her for what she'd done. And that he was leaving. Last time four years had passed before he'd returned to the States.

She was saved from Savannah probing deeper by her cell phone going off. Something was probably going on in the CVICU where they needed her to return to the floor. She grabbed her phone, readying to head back to the unit.

"Hey, Mom, how are things there?" she said instead when it was her mother's voice she heard.

"They aren't here."

Chrissie's heart shriveled up in her chest. "What do you mean?"

"Joss isn't here. Trace isn't here. There's not a car here. He's taken him, Chrissie. He's taken Joss!"

Her mother's panic matched her own.

Trace had taken Joss. She'd only left him alone with their son for a few hours and he'd done the unthinkable. He'd taken Joss.

All the blood in Chrissie's body migrated to pound in her temples.

What did she do? Call the police and report that her son had been kidnapped?

No. First thing she needed to do was call Trace. To see if there was a perfectly logical explanation for why he and Joss weren't at the house, why he hadn't let her know they were leaving.

"I've got to go, Mom. I'm going to call Trace to see why they aren't there."

At her comment, Savannah's eyes widened.

"I'll let you know what I find out," Chrissie promised her mother, hanging up the phone, then meeting her friend's eyes. "He's not there. He and Joss are gone. Oh, God. They're not there."

Her insides were crumbling and Savannah moved to put her arm around her shoulder as

Chrissie's hand shook. Tears blinded her as she went to type in Trace's number.

But before she could get the first number punched in, her phone rang again.

"Trace! Where are you?" she demanded when she saw who the caller was.

"He's going to be okay."

His first words didn't reassure her. Nor did the loud whine of the siren coming over the phone.

"What's wrong with Joss? Where are you? Why aren't you at the house? My mom just called to say no one was at the house. What have you done?" Chrissie's legs went weak and she grabbed hold of the table to keep from falling from her chair as she demanded, "I knew I shouldn't have left him with you. What did you let happen to my baby?"

CHAPTER FOURTEEN

TRACE WINCED AT Chrissie's question. Not that he didn't deserve her accusation and so much more.

How could he have been so blind to what was happening? He was a doctor and he'd missed all the signs. Had ignored what his son had told him because he'd thought Joss just didn't want to go with him.

Then again, Kerry had died on his watch too. If he'd been paying closer attention, maybe he'd have noticed she was slipping, maybe her doctors could have bought her more time before the cancer stole her last breath.

With Joss's not feeling well and lack of cooperation, texting Chrissie's mom had completely slipped Trace's mind. Which meant Chrissie had likely been in a panic before he'd said the first word. What he had to tell her wasn't going to help matters.

"We're on our way to your hospital by ambulance. We think Joss has appendicitis." We being him and the paramedics who'd been waiting where the train had made an emergency stop. "I wanted to spend time with him and took him to ride the trains. We were going to ride, have lunch, and then be home long before you got off work. But things didn't go as planned and Joss got sick," he rushed out. "We should be there in—" he glanced at the paramedic monitoring Joss "—four minutes max."

Once Trace had realized what was going on, his brain had finally kicked into gear and he'd called 911 as he'd stripped Joss's dirty T-shirt and shorts off him. He hadn't bothered to redress him, not with his temperature spiked so high.

A couple on the train with their older boys had moved up and offered to help clean up, as had the conductor, who'd radioed the engineer to alert him as to what was happening in one of his passenger cars. Trace hadn't cared about the mess. All he'd cared about was the little boy who'd been sobbing in pain, asking over and over for his mother as the train had rushed forward to where Joss could be transferred to an ambulance.

While Trace held his hand, the paramedics had started an intravenous line and given Joss something to ease his discomfort as they rushed him toward the emergency room.

Chrissie chewed his ear some more and Trace let her for a moment, knowing he deserved her wrath. Then, he cut the call short so he could focus on his son, whose hand he still held.

"Mommy," Joss mumbled in his sedated state.

"I called her, buddy. She'll be waiting for you in the emergency room."

She was.

The moment the back of the ambulance opened, Chrissie came rushing out of the hospital.

"Oh, God," she moaned, her gaze assessing Joss on the stretcher as the paramedics unloaded him from the ambulance. "Joss, Mommy's here," she told him, rushing alongside the stretcher as they wheeled Joss into the hospital.

Trace kept up with the stretcher as well.

"Mommy's here," she told Joss over and over until the emergency-room nurse hugged Chrissie, pulling her back from the stretcher. "No," she protested.

"They need to do imaging. You can't be in the room. I'm sorry."

Trace wanted to argue, wanted to say he and Chrissie could go in with their son, but he knew to do so would slow down everything.

"Come on, Chrissie. Let them do their job so Joss can get the best care as quickly as possible."

Never had Trace felt a bigger failure than when Chrissie turned to him.

"Don't you tell me what to do when it comes to my son," she hissed at him. "I never should have left him with you. Never."

Chrissie felt Trace's flinch all the way to her core, but she couldn't retract her words. Just as she couldn't retract the things she'd said to him when he'd called her.

Seemed she was always saying something she wished she could take back when it came to Trace.

But the sound of the siren, knowing her baby

was hurt, the sight of Joss's little body lying on that stretcher, had undone her.

She liked to think of herself as an empathetic, compassionate nurse, but never had she experienced anything to prepare her for the pain and fear of seeing her child like that.

She'd lashed out at Trace.

Maybe because she'd already been in a panic, thinking Trace had taken her son, just as her father had run with her.

He hadn't. He'd wanted to take Joss for a train ride. He'd wanted to give their son a fun day and had had no intentions of kidnapping him.

But Chrissie couldn't erase the devastation she'd felt at her mother's words that no one was at her house and she'd taken all her emotions out on Trace.

That had been an hour ago. Or a day ago. Or a week ago. Time had no meaning to Chrissie and with the way each second dragged by she'd believe years had passed since her son had been taken for emergency surgery for a ruptured appendix.

She, Trace, her mother, and Savannah had been left in a surgery waiting area where the walls kept closing in around Chrissie. She had cried so many tears on Savannah's shoulder that no doubt Charlie would think his wife had been caught in a downpour by the time she finally made it home.

Her poor mother was almost as big a mess as she was that she hadn't gotten to Chrissie's house earlier, that somehow this was all her fault for having run late.

Her mother had avoided Trace, other than to glare at him as if he were the devil, but Savannah had introduced herself, had hugged him, too, trying to ease his distress.

But not Chrissie.

Chrissie couldn't bring herself to even look at him.

Because looking at him hurt.

Hurt because Joss looked like him.

Hurt because she'd verbally attacked him.

Hurt because she wanted so much more than what they had.

Hurt because he'd allowed this to happen to their son.

Logically, she knew he hadn't *allowed* Joss to get sick, that appendicitis could just as easily have happened while he'd been in her care, while he'd been in Trace and her mother's care at her house. But it hadn't. It had happened while he'd been in Trace's care away from their house when Trace shouldn't have taken him anywhere.

How long had Joss's belly hurt? Had he been trying to be brave in front of his father? Had he cried and Trace ignored him? Had the pain and rupture hit suddenly?

How much longer was this surgery going to take?

She prayed and prayed. Over and over. *Please, please, please, let Joss be okay.*

When she and Trace were called to a consult room, Chrissie could barely walk, but she refused his offered hand.

She couldn't touch him, couldn't feel, could only focus on Joss.

"How is he?" she asked the nurse showing them to the room.

"I'm sorry. I honestly don't know any news on your son. I was buzzed and asked to put you in the consult room for Dr. Rodriguez."

If something bad had happened, the nurse would know, right?

Then again, why wouldn't they have told a patient's family straight away that all was okay so they could quit worrying?

"Joss needs a blood transfusion," the doctor said immediately upon entering the consult room. "He has a rare blood type and we, unfortunately, have had a run on that type today. I need to type and cross you both for a match."

"I'm B positive," Chrissie said, knowing her type from having donated at multiple blood drives over the years.

"It's me," Trace said, fighting the guilt inside him that he'd allowed this to happen to his son, that even now his blood was delaying his son's care. "I'm O Rh negative."

He was a much sought-after donor as any blood

type could receive his blood, but when it came to him receiving blood his options were limited to only someone who was an exact match. Something that had been problematic and almost cost him his life in Yemen after his injuries. Apparently, he'd passed that along to his son.

"Take whatever you need from me," he offered. He'd give every drop to save his son. Anything to help Joss. Anything to wipe the agony from Chrissie's face.

Seeing her pain, hearing her sobs, as they'd waited on news of their son had torn his insides to bits. Had brought memories of Kerry and when she'd passed to the forefront of his mind. Memories of Bud and Agnes mourning their daughter. Memories of Trace's own heart breaking at the loss of the first girl he'd loved. Guilt that he'd been there when she'd passed, and that he'd felt a failure ever since, that he should have been able to do something to save her.

Wasn't that why he'd become a doctor? So he could save people? Yet no matter how many he saved, there were so many more he couldn't.

He'd not even been able to spend a day alone with his son without something happening to him.

His gaze cut to Chrissie's red-rimmed eyes, her swollen face, and emotion swamped him. If Joss didn't pull through, she would never forgive him.

If Joss didn't pull through, Trace would never forgive himself.

* * *

Once Joss was in recovery, the hospital staff allowed Chrissie and Trace back to see him.

Trace felt the curious stares. No wonder. Chrissie worked here. Anyone who knew her knew she was a single mom, yet here he was, claiming to be Joss's father, giving blood.

Claiming to be Joss's father.

He *was* his father.

He hadn't needed a DNA test. Joss's eyes had been enough to convince him. If he had needed more proof, Joss's blood type would have been all he'd have needed.

"Joss, baby, Mommy is here," Chrissie cooed over and over in a soft voice as she held Joss's hand and waited for him to fully wake up.

His lashes fluttered.

"Mommy's here," she repeated.

"Mommy?" Joss said, his voice hoarse and weak. "My belly hurts."

Trace's insides wrenched. How many times had Joss said that earlier in the day? Too many. He'd been so determined to prove that he could take care of his son by himself and all he'd done was prove the complete opposite. He'd been wrong to take Joss to the train station, to go around Chrissie's wishes. So very wrong.

"Yes, baby. You had surgery on your belly. It's going to hurt for a while, but then it'll be all better," she promised.

Joss's eyes closed back.

"How's he doing?" Dr. Rodriguez asked, coming into the recovery area. "My partner did his operation, but he's caught me up on the details."

"Still trying to wake up," Chrissie told him. "But you just missed him opening his eyes."

"Poor thing," the surgeon commiserated. "He's going to hurt when he wakes up."

"Yeah, he said his belly was hurting when he opened his eyes a minute ago," Chrissie empathized, stroking her fingertip over Joss's hand.

"Tough little guy—he had to be in a lot of pain prior to the rupture."

Yeah, he had been but his obtuse father had thought he just didn't want to spend the day with him and had been determined he was going to anyway.

Trace shook his head. How could he have been so stupid? So blind? So selfish?

His son could have died because of him.

Joss would have been better off if Chrissie hadn't told Trace.

He was leaving in less than two weeks. He shouldn't have come to Chattanooga. He would go back overseas where he could help others rather than interfere where he wasn't wanted or needed.

"Where's my daddy?"

At Joss's question, Chrissie looked behind her to where Trace had been standing. The recovery room bay was now empty except for the nurse standing ten or so feet away at a computer where she was charting.

"Your daddy was here just a few minutes ago, baby," she assured a droopy-eyed Joss. "He's been very worried about you."

She wasn't sure where Trace had stepped away to, but was sure he'd be back soon.

Only he wasn't.

Not that evening. Not that night. Not the next morning. Not the next evening or night.

Not the following day when Joss was released to go home.

Chrissie had called his cell phone, but it had repeatedly gone straight to voicemail. She'd left a dozen messages, but hadn't heard back from him.

Not once.

A week ago, Joss had never met his father.

Now, he kept asking about where he was, obviously missed him, and Chrissie didn't know what to tell him.

Was Trace coming back or had he left for good?

In just over a week, he'd be gone to Africa.

Anger built inside her that he'd just left without saying goodbye, without anything.

Joss had been home for two days, was doing great, and Chrissie had difficulty focusing on anything other than that Trace had come into their lives, made an impression on Joss, then just left without even telling him goodbye.

Yes, she'd been angry with him over taking Joss without her knowledge or permission, had lashed out at him, but to just disappear without saying goodbye to their son? How could he do that?

Had he already gone back overseas?

How dared he? How dared he come into her house and give them a glimpse of how things could have been had their situation been different, then just leave without a word?

How dared he think she'd just let him walk away without a backward glance?

Because she wouldn't.

Not without giving him a piece of her mind.

Which was just as well as she'd already given him a piece of her heart.

Trace's mother lifted her wineglass to her lips and took a more than generous sip. "How is it best for a child not to know his grandparents?"

Trace grimaced. He'd hated telling his parents about Joss for fear they'd contact Chrissie, but he'd not wanted to put Bud and Agnes in the awkward position of knowing his parents had a grandchild they knew nothing about. They'd looked pretty pleased right up until he'd asked them to stay away from Chrissie and Joss.

"It just is," he finally said, taking a sip of his

drink. He didn't expect his parents to understand, just prayed they'd respect his wishes.

"Do you really think we're such horrible parents, Trace? After all, we raised you and I've always believed you turned out okay."

"You thought wrong," he corrected his mother.

"Hogwash," Agnes spoke up from across the table from Trace. "You're seriously going back overseas because Joss had a bout of appendicitis?"

"I was already scheduled to go back overseas, and he didn't just have a bout of appendicitis. He almost died."

"Because of something that was completely beyond your control," Agnes told him.

"I should have known something more was going on with him."

Just as he should have known something more was going on with Kerry the day she died.

"Really? Because a three-year-old conveys what's going on inside him that well?" Agnes challenged.

Trace let out a long sigh. Agnes and Bud loved him. As much as he didn't agree with them on most accounts, his parents loved him, too. He wasn't going to win this battle.

"All I'm asking is that you don't interfere in Chrissie and Joss's life. Nothing beyond that, especially not these accolades of why I'm not at fault that Joss almost died. I know what I did."

What he'd done was be so caught up in what *he*

wanted, in wanting to *make* his son love him and want to spend time with him, that he'd almost let him die.

Chrissie had been right not to trust him with Joss's care.

Bud and Agnes shouldn't have trusted him to sit with Kerry that day.

Agnes's phone rang and, glancing at the number, she excused herself and left the table to take the call.

"Trace, I think you're making a mistake stepping away from your son," his father said from the head of the table.

"It's my mistake to make." The mistake had been going to Chrissie's and meeting Joss in the first place.

"That boy is the heir to my fortune," Trace's father spoke up as if that was the perfect argument.

"Chrissie doesn't want your fortune. She just wants Joss and he's better off with her."

"Son, I try to stay out of matters that aren't really my business, but I agree with your dad on this," Bud interjected. "You need to be a part of the boy's life."

"That isn't an option." His being a part of Joss's life had almost cost Joss's life. "I'm leaving and won't be back in the States for at least six months."

"Staying is an option. You just have to choose not to go." This came from Trace's father again.

Trace's mother took another sip of her wine.

"We want you to stay. We've always wanted you to stay. You know that."

Trace wondered why he'd put himself through this torture. Why had he agreed to dinner with his parents and Bud and Agnes?

Because other than the two people he'd left behind in Chattanooga, these four were the most important people in his life.

Because they loved him.

Just as he loved them.

Only…only he'd shut them out since Kerry had died. All of them to some degree. But mostly his parents.

Because Kerry dying had hurt and no matter how much money his father threw at him afterward, nothing could bring her back. After a while he'd started feeling suffocated by everyone's attempts to make his life better and he'd left for medical school, so no one else would die on his watch, and then he'd opted to join DAW.

Because he'd needed space between him and those he loved. Why? Had he been afraid to feel?

Was he still afraid to feel?

"Trace?" Agnes said, coming back into the room, her expression grim. "That was Chrissie. Joss needs you in Chattanooga."

"What?" He rose from the table, Agnes's worried expression immediately putting him on alert.

"Joss needs you. Now. Apparently he has some rare blood type and…" Agnes's voice trailed off.

That Agnes wouldn't meet his eyes escalated Trace's fear.

He'd been in touch with Joss's doctor every day. The man had his cell number and instructions to call if there were any changes. Joss had been doing well, had been home for a couple of days. What had happened?

He should call Chrissie. If Joss needed him, his blood, he had to go.

Trace's father stood. "I'll have the helicopter here in fifteen minutes and arrange for a car to meet you in Chattanooga."

"I… Yes, that would be best." He needed to get there as quickly as possible.

Not that they'd let him donate again this quickly. In which case…

"Actually—" he turned to his father, who shared his rare blood type "—can you go with me?"

His dad gave him a startled look. "Me? You want me to go?"

"I may need you there. Joss may need you."

"Then let's go."

Chrissie's phone buzzed.

"He's on his way."

"Wow." She hadn't been sure Agnes could pull off getting Trace to come back to Chattanooga to talk, but Agnes had assured her he would. When she'd called Trace's godmother she'd just been going after an address and to make sure Trace was still in Atlanta.

"His dad is with him," Agnes continued.

"His dad? Why is Trace's dad coming with him?"

"Long story." Agnes gave a little laugh. "Trace may have misunderstood something I said and thought Joss needed another blood transfusion."

"What?" Then why Trace was headed to Chattanooga clicked. "Agnes, when you said you'd make sure he came back, I didn't realize you were going to deceive him." Chrissie's heart sank. "I don't feel good about that. I've deceived him too much already."

"I didn't say Joss needed a blood transfusion. Besides, that boy's pride didn't need to get in his way."

That boy was a handsome grown man who Chrissie was angry at and yet…

"Oh, Agnes, he's coming because he's worried about Joss."

Which meant he wasn't coming for her, but for their son.

Which was okay.

If she had to choose, wasn't that what she'd pick? For Trace to be concerned about his son? For him to be there if Joss needed him? Obviously if he was on his way, he would be there for Joss.

Trace was on his way!

"You have to let him know Joss isn't in any danger. He's recovering wonderfully." She didn't want Trace worrying. She could only imagine the horror he must be experiencing.

"He'll be at your house any moment and you can tell him then."

"Any moment?" She'd thought she'd have a couple of hours to mentally prepare what she wanted to say.

"They took his dad's helicopter."

"His dad has a helicopter?"

Agnes laughed. "Oh, honey, you really have no clue, do you?"

Chrissie tried not to be insulted but wasn't sure she succeeded. "What am I supposed to say to him?"

"Now, that's something only you know. I'd guess a good place to start would be why you called me to get his information."

"If he's worried that Joss needs a blood transfusion, wouldn't he go to the hospital instead of here?"

Agnes laughed again. "You underestimate me. The car meeting them in Chattanooga knows where to bring them."

Them. As in Trace and his father.

"Agnes, Trace and I can't talk with his father with us."

"I know that, but you also need someone to watch Joss."

"Trace's dad is going to watch Joss? Isn't he like some kind of uptight businessman?"

"That's how some see him."

"But not you?"

"Not ever. He's a good man who is excited at the prospect of meeting his grandson."

"I just got Joss to bed, Agnes. He's still recovering."

"Fine. I'll call and let Randolph know he's to leave with the car."

Chrissie responded to Agnes, said goodbye to the woman, but couldn't have repeated what she'd said. Her mind was racing.

Trace was going to be there any moment.

What was she going to say to him?

The truth? That she and Joss had missed him? That they wanted him in their lives? That she was sorry for the things she'd said, done? That she knew Joss's appendicitis wasn't his fault?

That she'd attacked him because of her own inner beast that had worried he'd kidnapped their son?

He hadn't. He'd only wanted to love Joss, to get their son to open up to him and love him back.

Would he think her crazy? Selfish, perhaps, if they kept him from leaving to serve the world's poor, sick and injured?

Maybe she was selfish but she didn't want him to go back overseas. She wanted him here. With her. With Joss.

A car pulled in her drive and she went to the front door, not wanting Trace to knock in case it woke Joss. They needed to talk without their son overhearing.

She watched him get out of an expensive-looking black sedan, lean back down to say something to whomever still sat in the backseat. His father, she supposed. Looking confused, Trace closed the car door and headed toward the house. When the car pulled away, he paused, frowned, then met her gaze.

What if he was angry Agnes had sent him on false pretenses? How much did it even cost to have a helicopter bring you?

"Chrissie," he said, stepping onto the porch.

"Joss is fine," she blurted out.

Looking a bit dazed, he flexed his jaw. "That's what my father told me right before we pulled into your driveway."

She nodded. "Agnes said she was going to call him."

"You lied to her?"

"No," she quickly denied. "I called for your address, to make sure you hadn't left yet. Nothing more. She said she'd have you come to me. I assumed she'd talk you into it."

"He doesn't need to be dragged around so soon after his surgery."

"He's doing great. Played almost normal today."

He glanced past her into the house. "Where is he?"

"Asleep. He was tired, so I bathed him and put him to bed about twenty minutes ago."

"Can I see him?"

"Of course." The night he'd shown up at her house, insisting to see Joss, flashed through her mind. "He's missed you, Trace. So much."

His eyes cut to her. "Don't say that."

"Why?"

His jaw clenched. "Because it's not true."

"It is true. He's asked about you repeatedly. He wants to know where you are."

Trace took a deep breath. "What'd you tell him?"

"That you had to go home to Atlanta."

Trace nodded. He had had to go to Atlanta. Or so he'd told himself. Mainly, he'd had to get away because he'd felt such guilt over Joss. Like such a failure to his son.

"I've missed you, too."

Chrissie's words cut into his thoughts.

"Why?"

She gave a trembling smile. "Why not?"

It wasn't much of an answer, but she stepped aside and motioned for him to enter her house. He did so before she changed her mind. Before he changed his mind and took off after his father's hired car.

"You can go to his room if you want."

Her voice was wobbly and Trace found himself turning to look at her instead.

"I leave next week."

She nodded as if she understood, but he wasn't sure she did. Still, he needed to see Joss, to reassure himself that he was okay. Since Agnes's dramatic implication, he'd had a sick feeling in his stomach and he needed to see Joss to convince himself that he really was okay.

His nightlight illuminating his precious face, Joss slept on his car bed, snuggled up in his covers, and looking at peace with the world.

Just seeing him wasn't enough.

Trace went to the bed, sat on the edge, and touched Joss's face, brushing his finger over his soft cheek.

The little boy's eyes opened and Trace felt guilt for waking him.

"Daddy?"

His heart squeezed.

"I'm here, Joss." He touched Joss's fingers, then held his hand in his.

"Where did you go?"

"Atlanta."

"That's where Mommy said you went." Joss yawned, scooted up in the bed. "Can I go to Atlanta with you, too?"

Trace's heart swelled to the point he thought it might explode. But then he recalled that he'd almost let this child, his son, die.

That he'd been the last person with Kerry before she'd gotten so sick and died.

That he was leaving and would be gone for months.

"I'd never take you away from your mommy, Joss. She would miss you."

"We could bring her, too." Another big yawn, then he settled back onto his pillow. "She'd like Atlanta."

Trace wasn't so sure about that.

"I'm sorry I got sick."

"You couldn't help getting sick, Joss. I know that."

"You went away."

His words gutted Trace. Was that what he had thought?

"Not because you'd been sick," he assured. "Never that."

Only, was that true? Or had memories of Kerry and guilt played into his having left?

"I'm better now," Joss told him with heavy eyes. "Lots better."

He started to respond, but realized Joss's eyes had closed and he'd dozed back off. Quietly, Trace stood, turned to leave Joss's room and noticed Chrissie, crying, in the doorway.

She waited until they were both back in the living room, then said, "I want you in his life, Trace. He wants you in his life. Whenever you're home, between your assignments, whenever it's safe for him and me to visit you, we want you in our lives."

Heart pounding, he shook his head. "It's too complicated."

Staring at him from where she stood just in front of him, she frowned. "What's too complicated? You and me?"

"I meant him. Me. Everything."

"I don't understand."

"I shouldn't have taken him away from here that day, or even attempted to watch him on my own. You were right. I've never been good at taking care of someone."

She shook her head. "No, I was wrong. You should have been with him. You have just as much right to look after him as I do. Please forgive me for thinking otherwise. What happened wasn't your fault."

He shook his head. "Thank you for taking care of him, Chrissie."

She sucked in a deep breath and stared up at him. "You're leaving aren't you?"

She made it sound as if that were something horrible. He knew better. "I can't stay."

"Please don't go."

"Because of what Joss said?"

She shook her head, then took a deep breath and stepped to him, put her hand on his cheek. "Because of you and me."

"There is no 'you and me,'" he reminded her.

There wasn't. Just two beautiful weekends that had been like fairy-tale blips in reality.

She flinched, then straightened her shoulders. "I don't believe you, Trace. There's been a 'you and me' from the moment I first met you four years ago and I thought you were the most attractive man I'd ever met. I wanted you then," she admitted. She took a deep breath. "I want you now."

With that, she stood on her tiptoes and kissed him.

What was she doing? Chrissie wondered for the hundredth time. She shouldn't be kissing Trace.

Yes, she should, an inner voice argued. She should be kissing him every day for the rest of her life. Not that that was what he wanted.

He must not even want her anymore because he wasn't returning her kiss.

Then he was.

Not just returning her kiss but taking control of the kiss. Kissing her hard and full and with need.

A need she welcomed because she needed him.

Between kisses, he shook his head. "I'm no good for you and Joss."

She palmed his cheeks, making him look at her. "Why would you say that?"

"Because of what happened."

"Trace, his appendix ruptured. That wasn't your fault. I'm sorry for what I said at the hospital. I was scared, and wrong, and shouldn't have said any of those nasty things because they weren't true. I know that now. You got Joss the help he needed. You got him to the hospital. You did what needed to be done and our son is in there in his bed, healthy and sleeping."

"I'm his father. It's my job to protect him. I didn't."

"Ha. I second-guess myself when it comes to raising him every single day. I do the best I can, but I know there are so many things that I just do the best I can and hope it's enough. Now I know it's not. Like when I said I didn't want him to stay alone with you. I was wrong, Trace."

"This isn't the first time this has happened, Chrissie. I let Kerry die, too."

Horror gripped her. "Bud and Agnes's daughter? I thought she died of cancer?"

Raking his fingers through his hair, Trace then massaged his temple. "I was the last person with her before she slipped into a coma. She never woke back up."

Wondering at the pain inside him, Chrissie sank onto the sofa with a plop. "What happened?"

"She was on hospice, was dying. Someone sat with her around the clock. One minute she was talking with me, the next she closed her eyes, and never woke back up. I thought she was sleeping but she was dying."

"That wasn't your fault, Trace. No more than what happened to Joss was your fault."

"He told me his belly hurt and I thought he just wanted you so I kept trying to distract him. I forced him to leave here and to go with me. I never gave credence that his belly might really hurt."

She grimaced. "You didn't know."

"I should have. You would have." He paced across the room, turned, gave her a pained look. "I'll give you money."

She felt sucker punched. "I don't want money."

"What do you want?"

Time for the truth. It wasn't going to be easy, but she had to do it. Had to say it.

"You."

He just stared at her.

"Did you hear me, Trace? I want you. In my life, my house, my bed," she continued, letting her emotions pour out of her. "I want you. All of you."

"I..." His voice trailed off. "Why?"

"Are you kidding me?" When he didn't respond she knew he was serious. "Because..." She could tell him how wonderful she thought he was, how handsome, how sexy, how smart and funny. But none of that was what came out of her mouth. "Because I've never stopped wanting you and I don't think I ever will."

His gaze searched hers. "What are you saying?"

She gulped back the big bundle of nerves threatening to choke her. "I'm in love with you, Trace."

"I don't know what to say."

Which wasn't what she wanted to hear. Her heart fell.

"You don't have to say anything." She turned away from him, not willing to let him see the big fat tears welling up in her eyes. "I just needed to tell you how I felt, that I wanted you in my and Joss's life. I was so angry at you for just leaving us. There's so much I haven't told you." She turned to face him, scared to admit what she was about to say, words she really hadn't spoken once social services and the police had finished questioning her all those years ago. "My father kidnapped me from my mother. I thought you were doing the same thing that day with Joss. That's why I couldn't hold in my emotions and hurt and fear. I'd wanted to trust you, Trace, and I'd been afraid to, and felt you'd confirmed my worst fears."

His look of horror reflected all she already knew deep in her heart about the man standing in front of her.

"I just wanted to spend the day with him, just me and him. I wanted him to have fun with me, to enjoy being with me, to need me."

He winced. "I shouldn't have taken him. You were right to lash out at me."

"You weren't stealing him from me, Trace. You were trying to forge a relationship with him that my paranoia was interfering with."

"He's yours, Chrissie. Is that what you want to

hear me say? You're his mother and he needs you. I know that."

"He's yours, too, Trace. You're his father and he needs you, too. I know that now," she admitted, believing it with all her heart. "That's why I called Agnes, because I wanted to come to Atlanta to tell you how sorry I am, to beg you to forgive me for not telling you about him, for not trusting you with him, for all the mistakes I've made." She put her hands over her face, wiped at the wetness. "I'm sorry Agnes tricked you into coming here."

Trace was nothing like her father. He was the best man she'd ever met. She'd created issues where there had been none, had let fear poison her judgment. How could Trace ever forgive her?

How could Joss ever forgive her when she explained to him that his daddy had left because of her mistakes?

"I'm not."

Chrissie lifted her gaze to Trace's, waited for him to tell her how foolish she was, how he could never forgive how deceitful and mistrusting she'd been.

"I love you, Chrissie," he said instead, almost dropping her to the floor. "Thinking of you, of being with you in Atlanta is what got me through the hell I went through overseas. When I saw you again a few weeks ago, you were as sweet as I remembered. I'm sorry for what your father did to you, Chrissie. I can't even imagine the hell you and your mother must have gone through. I'd never do that to you or Joss. Never."

Chrissie's insides shook at the sincerity in his voice, at the sincerity shining in his eyes as he gazed down at her.

"He's beautiful, Chrissie. I'd say the most beautiful thing I'd ever seen, but I'd be lying." He cupped her face. "I'm looking at the most beautiful thing I've ever seen. You."

He kissed her again. This time slower, more passionately, and she kissed him back with her all, not quite believing the things he'd said.

"Am I dreaming?" she asked, wondering if she should pinch herself. "Are you really here?"

He brushed his thumb across her cheek. "If you're dreaming, I'm having the same dream."

"So what happens now?" she asked, not quite sure what everything they'd said up to that point meant.

"What do you want to happen?"

His question was a no-brainer. She didn't have to think on it even a millisecond. She knew exactly what she wanted.

"I want you to stay here, Trace, with me and Joss forever." She took a deep breath. "But I know you're committed to leaving. Soon. If the need is within you to live in some war-torn, impoverished country, we'll go with you." She met his gaze. "That is, if you want us to."

"You know I do." When he kissed her again,

she had to agree. She did know. It was there. In his kiss. In his touch. In the way he was looking at her.

"But maybe it's time I rethink going back overseas."

"A week before leaving? I don't want you to give up something you love for me."

"If I left you and Joss, I would be giving up things I love. I'm not going back with DAW."

She couldn't believe what he was saying. She wanted this man happy, to do whatever it took to make his life complete.

"I'm glad, but I was serious," she assured him. "We'll go wherever you are."

"Chattanooga isn't so far away from Atlanta, Chrissie. Maybe we could spend time in both cities. That way Joss could know both sets of his grandparents."

Happiness burst through her whole being.

"And his grand-godparents," she added, thinking of Bud and Agnes.

"They'll spoil him. They've been waiting for years for me to give them grandchildren." He gave her a serious look. "They'll insist upon more."

"More? You mean—?" Chrissie's breath caught "—you want more children? But I thought…"

"The thought terrifies me in many ways, but, yes, I want more kids. With you. Brothers and sisters for Joss."

She threw her arms around his neck and kissed his cheek. "Oh, Trace. I do love you!"

He laughed. "Good. Now about those brothers and sisters…"

EPILOGUE

"No, DON'T YOU dare pick up that box of supplies," Agnes ordered when Chrissie bent to pick up a box.

Not that Chrissie had actually done much bending.

Her body just wasn't cooperating these days. Not with her belly in the way.

Her very round, very pregnant belly.

"You sound like my husband," she accused, wanting to help more than she knew they were going to let her.

"Yeah? I hear he's an amazing man," Trace said, coming up behind her and patting her bottom, then giving her a more serious look. "How are you holding up?"

"Fine."

"You're not too tired?"

"Trace, the event hasn't even started yet."

"I just think you should have sat this year out and stayed at my parents' place with Joss."

"And encroached on his time with his Gramps and Grammie?" she asked. "I don't think so. They've been looking forward to taking him to the Atlanta Aquarium for weeks. He loves it so much! I can't believe your dad arranged a sleepover there."

Trace grinned. "I told you they'd spoil him."

But his voice was light, happy. Although she knew Trace and his father hadn't seen eye to eye most of his adult life, they'd come to a peace from the time they'd flown to Chattanooga together, thinking they were going to save Joss's life.

Instead, they'd saved Chrissie.

Saved her from a life with part of her heart missing.

"Just as you spoil me," she accused, wrapping her arms around his neck, but unable to pull him as close as she'd like due to her belly between them.

He leaned forward, dropped a kiss on her lips, then cupped her stomach. "You're the one who has spoiled me."

"You just keep thinking that and I'll know the truth," she teased, as she often did. The truth was, they were both spoiled by the happiness they'd found together.

A happiness that came from deep within and shined outward for the whole world to see and feel its warmth.

A happiness that was love.

The kind that would last forever.

And did.

* * * * *